CHASING SHADOWS

A SHELBY BELGARDEN MYSTERY

CHASING SHADOWS

Valerie Sherrard

A BOARDWALK BOOK
A MEMBER OF THE DUNDURN GROUP
TORONTO

Editor: Barry Jowett
Copy-Editor: Andrea Pruss
Design: Jennifer Scott
Printer: AGMV Marquis

National Library of Canada Cataloguing in Publication Data

Sherrard, Valerie
    Chasing shadows/Valerie Sherrard.

ISBN 1-55002-502-3

I. Title.

PS8587.H3867C43 2004   jC813'.6   C2003-907198-7

1   2   3   4   5   08   07   06   05   04

We acknowledge the support of the **Canada Council for the Arts** and the **Ontario Arts Council** for our publishing program. We also acknowledge the financial support of the **Government of Canada** through the **Book Publishing Industry Development Program** and **The Association for the Export of Canadian Books**, and the **Government of Ontario** through the **Ontario Book Publishers Tax Credit** program.

Care has been taken to trace the ownership of copyright material used in this book. The author and the publisher welcome any information enabling them to rectify any references or credit in subsequent editions.

J. Kirk Howard, President

Printed and bound in Canada.✆   Printed on recycled paper.   www.dundurn.com

Dundurn Press	Gazelle Book Services Limited	Dundurn Press
8 Market Street	White Cross Mills	2250 Military Road
Suite 200	Hightown, Lancaster, England	Tonawanda NY
Toronto, Ontario, Canada	LA1 4X5	U.S.A. 14150
M5E 1M6		

Dedicated with love to
my husband, partner,
and best friend,
Brent.
A man among men.

CHAPTER ONE

Mom glanced up from the sheets of paper that were spread over the kitchen table. They were covered with lists — mostly of food items — and she added to them as new ideas came to her.

"What colours of balloons will we have?"

"None. I don't want any balloons."

It's funny how Mom can manage to summon the most forlorn looks over such trivial things. She got this pathetic hangdog expression on her face, as though I'd just announced I was quitting school and joining a terrorist group.

Let her overreact, I thought, *I'm holding my ground.* After all, it's *my* birthday. And Mom gets completely out of control with balloons. The last time I had a party she must have blown up hundreds of them. They were *everywhere*, hanging from the ceilings and doorways, stuck to furniture. The house looked like it was decorated for a small child's party. It was totally embarrassing.

"But they're so pretty," Mom said with her face all piled up.

"Still, I don't want any. Balloons are for kids." *I'm not giving in on this*, I decided. *It's only three days away; I can handle her acting dejected for that long.*

She sighed heavily and picked a piece of lint off her sweater. I steeled myself, figuring she'd try harder to persuade me.

"Oh, all right then." She shrugged in resignation. It surprised me that she was giving in so easily. "We'll just do something else. I know! I'll make up banners and hang streamers."

"What kind of banners?" I should have been suspicious, but then a girl likes to think her own mom can be trusted.

"The usual thing, like 'Happy Birthday.'" Her face was *way* too innocent. "And I'll make up some with a theme."

"Don't do anything dumb like sweet sixteen!" I said.

"Of course not. I have a much better idea. I'll do a 'Through the Years' theme. You know, with a collage of your pictures, from birth to now."

"You *can't* be serious!"

"Well, we have to have *some* decorations." She smiled sweetly, arching an eyebrow helplessly as if to ask what else she was supposed to do since I didn't want the balloons. "The picture of you in your bath when you were just a few months old is adorable. I'll do a big blow-up of that one beside a current shot, for over the living room archway."

I'd lost and I knew it.

"Okay, maybe a *few* balloons. But don't overdo it. And absolutely no pink!"

"Well, fuchsia …"

"No pink."

"Okay, okay. What kind of cake do you want?"

"Just something plain."

"You girls still at it?" Dad asked from the doorway. He barely had his nose in the kitchen. I guess he figured it wasn't safe to come around when Mom was in high gear planning a party. There was always the risk that he'd be roped into doing something, like the time Mom got him to make a big, sparkly sign for some ladies' meeting she was having. He'd had glitter clinging to him for days afterward, which had apparently earned him a good deal of teasing at work, as you can well imagine.

"We're almost through for now." Mom glanced up at him and smiled. My parents are always smiling at each other all lovey-dovey like. At their age, you'd think they'd know better. "Did you want something, dear?"

"Oh, no, don't worry about me. I'll just be quietly starving to death in the other room if anyone wants me."

"Goodness!" Mom glanced at her watch in alarm. "It's later than I realized." She stacked the papers together and laid them on top of the microwave. "I guess we lost track of time, planning for Shelby's party and all. I'll get dinner started right away."

"Or I could take my two gals out for dinner," Dad suggested. "We could try out that new restaurant downtown."

"I don't know." Mom hesitated. "I'd feel guilty. We always eat at The Water's Edge. Anyway, the owners of the new place aren't from Little River. It seems wrong not to give our business to Terry and Joy."

Terry and Joy Austers own The Water's Edge, which is the only restaurant around here that's kind of fancy inside. Or, at least, it was, until The Steak Place opened up a few months ago. The Austerses play canasta with my folks sometimes, so I knew Mom would feel disloyal eating somewhere else. At the same time, I could see that she was curious about the new restaurant, so I figured Dad would be able to convince her.

"Well, Darlene, I don't know. The owners of the new place came here and made a big investment to start up their business. That meant money in the town's economy. And they're employing locals. I don't think it would hurt to support them once in a while."

Mom's curiosity won out, and it was settled. A few moments later we'd gotten ready and were on our way.

As we drove, we passed Broderick's Gas Bar, where my boyfriend, Greg Taylor, works. He was busy washing a windshield, but he noticed us and waved and smiled. My stomach gave a happy little lurch, the way it always does when I see him. I blew him a kiss, and his hand reached up in the air like he was grabbing it.

"Nice catch," Dad grinned from the driver's seat. He doesn't miss much.

We reached The Steak Place in no time and were taken to a table by a tall, elegant-looking woman in a long black skirt and white blouse. I guessed she was one of the owners, since she wasn't familiar to me at all.

"Your waitress will be with you in just a moment," she said. She spoke with an accent, and she smiled pleasantly as she gave us menus and filled our water glasses.

Once we were seated I had a chance to look around at the place. It was nice, but not as big inside as I'd expected. There'd been a big fabric outlet there until a few years ago, when it had gone out of business. The place had sat empty until the end of February this year, when it had been bought and converted into a restaurant. It was finished and open for business by the first week of April.

"Wasn't this place bigger before?" I asked Mom. We'd shopped at the fabric store lots of times, and it had seemed enormous.

"It does look that way," Mom agreed looking around. "Of course, it was wide open then. The kitchen and restrooms would take up some space. Still, I'd think the dining area would be quite a bit bigger than this."

"Good evening." A young woman broke into our conversation. "I'm Nadine and I'll be your waitress tonight."

"Hi, Nadine," Dad answered. "The womenfolk here aren't ready to order yet. They're too busy looking the place over. Apparently they don't care if I collapse from hunger."

"My husband likes to exaggerate," Mom laughed. "Whatever you do, don't give him any sympathy."

"We were just noticing that it seems a lot smaller in here than it used to," I interjected.

"That's because they've sectioned off the back part for private parties, but it's not finished yet," she explained.

"Say, you're not, by any chance, little Nadine Gardiner are you?" Dad asked, looking at her more closely.

"Yes. Do I know you?"

"Your mom was my secretary at Stoneworks, years ago," Dad explained. "You were probably too young at the time to remember, though."

"No, I do!" Her face lit up. "I used go there after school until she got off work. You gave me candy and told me knock-knock jokes."

"So I did," Dad said, clearly pleased that she remembered him. "And here you are all grown up. How's your mother these days?"

"Great. She got married again a couple of years ago and moved to Dartmouth with her new husband."

"Well, you be sure to tell her I said hello."

"I will." Her eyes shone as she smiled at Dad. Then she told us she'd give us a few more minutes to look at the menu. As she said this, she gave Mom and me a stern look, as if to remind us that poor Dad was hungry and we should hurry up.

We were ready with our selections when she came back. Dad ordered prime rib while Mom and I chose chicken Caesar salads. Nadine brought over a wicker basket containing rolls and garlic bread and told us our meals wouldn't be long.

Dad was buttering a roll when he noticed the sign.

"Well, look over there, Shelby," he said, pointing. "You were talking about getting a job once you turned sixteen."

I turned and saw a notice that said "Kitchen Help Wanted" posted under the cash register.

Chapter Two

After we'd eaten, I told my folks I was going to look into the job for a kitchen helper.

"I'll go ask for an application while you two have your coffee," I said, standing up. They smiled encouragingly as I turned to head toward the cash register.

The lady who'd seated us when we first arrived was there. Something about her made me a bit nervous, though I can't quite explain why. Maybe it was just because she was a stranger to me. Or it could have been the way she was dressed, all elegant looking, and how she carried herself, so tall and thin. When I asked about the opening that was posted, she gave me a cool smile, the kind that stops at the mouth instead of spreading up to the eyes.

"I'm Lisa, the manager," she said. "Have you worked in a restaurant before?"

"No, ma'am. I'm just turning sixteen this week so I'm looking for my first job."

"I see." Another chilly smile. "Come with me."

Surprised that she wanted to interview me after finding out that I had no experience, I followed her into a small office beside the kitchen. She waved me into a chair and then perched, half sitting and half standing, against the desk.

"So, tell me something about yourself."

That threw me, let me tell you. I'd been expecting her to ask specific questions, like, did I know how to chop vegetables and do dishes and stuff. I cast about in my head for something to say.

"Uh, my name is Shelby Belgarden and I'm almost sixteen," I started off lamely, then remembered with some embarrassment that I'd just told her that only seconds before. "I'm in the tenth grade at school. I haven't worked before but I've done some babysitting, and I help Mom in the kitchen a lot."

She nodded without any sign of interest and said nothing. Instead, she seemed to be waiting for me to continue.

"I'm reliable and trustworthy," I added at last. My mouth was dry; I wished I could ask for a glass of water. "Oh, and I can work evenings and weekends for now, but the school year is finished in a couple of weeks. I'd be available any time during the summer holidays."

"All right, Shelby, that's fine."

I thought she was indicating that the interview was over. I was about to get up to leave the room when she spoke again. "The cook will tell you what you have to do."

With astonishment, I realized that she'd actually meant I was hired. I tried to look calm, so she wouldn't see how excited I was.

"Can you start right away?"

"Right away?" For a second I thought she wanted me to roll up my sleeves and head to the kitchen.

"This week?" She looked amused, as though she'd read my mind. "Saturday maybe?"

"Oh, uh, Saturday is my birthday. My mom has this big party planned." I felt like a fool, explaining that I couldn't come in for the first date she'd mentioned. "Everyone's already invited."

"Yes, the birthday. Sixteen." Her lips twisted in what seemed to be distaste. I couldn't tell if it was because I couldn't work on Saturday or because I was so young.

"Sorry."

"So then, Sunday?"

"Sure, Sunday would be fine."

"Come at ten o'clock. Black pants, white top. Hair must be tied back. Bring your social insurance number. We will see how it goes after a few weeks." She slid from the edge of the desk and reached the door in two quick strides. She pulled it open and waited for me to go out first.

I thanked her and hurried back to the table where Mom and Dad were waiting. They looked at me inquisitively.

I could picture Mom squealing and getting all excited at the news. Since there were quite a few other people around, I thought I'd spare myself that kind of scene.

"Well?" Mom asked before I'd sat all the way down.

"I'll tell you in the car."

"Oh, dear." Mom looked crestfallen. I guess she thought if I didn't want to say anything while we were still there, it hadn't gone well. She reached over and patted my hand. At the same time, she offered me a consoling look.

"Well, I'm ready to go whenever you girls are," Dad said, reaching for his wallet. We all got up, and he paid the bill and left a big tip for Nadine.

"You mustn't be discouraged," Mom told me as soon as we climbed into the car. "There are other places to work."

"I start Sunday," I answered.

"What? You mean you got the job?" Just as I'd expected, her voice rose in excitement. "My goodness, why didn't you say so right away?"

"I wanted it to be a private moment," I said hastily.

"Well, that's just wonderful! Isn't it wonderful, Randall?"

"It's real nice. Good for you, Shelby. Congratulations." Dad smiled at me in the rear-view mirror.

"Can you imagine," Mom went on, "our girl getting the *very first* job she applies for. How many young people can say that? Right on the spot like that too."

"Actually, I was only hired on a trial basis," I said quickly. "She said she'd see how it went for the first few weeks."

"Well, you'll do fine, dear. You have to think positive!"

"Yes, Mom." We were getting close to home, and I suddenly had an urge to escape from my mother's enthusiasm. Or maybe that was just an excuse I dreamed up because I wanted to see Greg.

"Uh, Dad, could you drop me off at Broderick's? I'd like to tell Greg about my job."

"Sure thing," Dad agreed. He turned in to the gas station when we reached it, and I hopped from the car and hurried inside.

Greg didn't notice me coming until I swung the door open. He was engrossed in his math textbook, and I knew he was studying for final exams, which were coming up the next week. When he looked up, his face broke into a wide smile.

"Hey! This is a nice surprise." He stood, setting the book on the counter. "What's up?"

"We just came from that new restaurant downtown — The Steak Place," I said breathlessly. "And guess what! I got a job there!"

"You didn't leave a whole lot of time for me to guess," Greg laughed. "Anyway, that's great. Are you going to be a waitress?"

"No, a kitchen helper. I think I probably have to peel potatoes and stuff like that. It's not the most glamorous job in the world, but at least I'll be making some money."

"Well, you'll be the cutest vegetable peeler in town."

"Yeah, that's what I've been longing to be known as — a cute vegetable peeler."

"Hey, it'll look great on your resumé. Besides, not everyone can land a really cool job right off the bat, like I did. I've been dreaming about pumping gas ever since I was a little kid. The only bad thing about it is how women are always coming on to me. I think it's because of the uniform."

"All that brown polyester *is* pretty sharp," I giggled.

"I bet it makes you want to kiss me." He nodded knowingly.

"Well, I *am* only human."

"No one would blame you if you couldn't help yourself." He leaned forward slightly, smiling.

If you want the truth, I didn't even try to resist.

Chapter Three

In spite of my warnings (and her promises) Mom went way overboard with the balloons. They were *everywhere*, hanging from light fixtures, doorways, and ceilings, stuck to walls, bursting out of vases in bloated bouquets, and just lying about the floor. The colour explosion was enough to hurt a person's eyes. At least none of them were pink, though some of the ones she insisted were burgundy looked suspiciously close to fuchsia to me.

I figured she must be afflicted with some kind of weird compulsive decorating disease and couldn't help herself, so I didn't complain. Besides, Greg had arrived before anyone else, and he thought the house looked great.

Greg's mom died a year ago, which gives him a bit of a different outlook on the insane things moms can do sometimes. I have to admit it helps me see my own mom in a softer light when she does something that irritates me — like she had with the balloons.

"The place looks amazing," Greg told Mom. "You must have spent hours and hours decorating."

"Oh, I didn't mind," she said, pleased. "Anything for my little girl."

For her little girl indeed! The truth is that *she's* the one who goes all crazy over stuff like this. Well, if it meant that much to her, I guessed I could just let her enjoy it and not mention that.

My best friend, Betts, was the next to arrive. Without even saying hello, she grabbed my arm and pulled me to a corner in the front hallway.

"Tell me you didn't invite Derek," she said, in a tone that sounded like she was issuing a command.

"Of course I did. He's your boyfriend, remember?"

"You mean he *was* my boyfriend," she said. "I ditched him this afternoon. He'd better not show up here tonight."

"But I thought everything was going great with you and Derek." As I spoke, I looked for signs that she might be teasing. Betts is pretty transparent most of the time, so I figured if she was making it up — for whatever reason — I'd be able to tell. Her face seemed normal to me, though, so it I decided it was true.

"We were okay until he decided to turn into a total jerk." Betts tossed her head back, her mouth pinched in a pout. This only lasted a few seconds, though, and then she snapped back to normal. Well, normal might not be quite the right word for Betts.

"Look at this place!" she squealed. "Your mom went *insane* with the balloons!"

"Yeah, I know." I was impatient to find out what had happened with Derek, and more guests would be coming any minute, making it impossible. Betts had been going out with him for months and they seemed really well-suited to each other. In fact, it was one of the longest relationships she'd ever had. The suddenness of the breakup was strange enough, but her apparent indifference was really unsettling.

"I mean, she must have bought every balloon in town," Betts giggled. "It looks like the balloon factory blew up in here."

"Betts!" I said sharply. "Never mind that right now. What happened with you and Derek?"

"Oh, that." She tried to look bored, as though the subject was of no interest to her whatsoever. "He's history."

"But *why*, Betts?" I'd never had so much trouble getting information out of her in all the years we'd been friends.

"We had a fight, a big one." She shrugged, like she

didn't care, but there was a barely perceptible tremble in her lip and a catch in her throat. "He said I was controlling, that I *always* have to have my own way, and that he can't even breathe when I'm ordering him around all the time."

Betts *is* a bit bossy at times, so I could kind of see Derek's point, but she's not *that* bad. Anyway, my main concern wasn't who was right, it was how Betts was feeling. It was starting to be pretty clear that she was putting on a brave front, probably on account of not wanting to spoil anything for me on my birthday.

"So you dumped him?" I asked, not really knowing what else to say.

"Yeah." She sounded miserable. It seemed the cover-up was crumbling fast.

"Well, was he upset about it?"

"I don't know. Anyway, who cares?" As she spoke, she tilted her chin up and smiled. Even if I hadn't known her well enough to see through that, the act she was trying to put on was contradicted by the tears suddenly brimming in her eyes.

"Oh, Betts, it'll be okay. I bet he feels worse than you do."

"Who says I feel bad?" she sniffed, then burst into sobs.

"Come on, let's go get some punch and not think about it right now," I said, putting my arm around her shoulder. "But you mark my words, you and Derek will be back together before I have my first full week in at work."

I'd hoped to distract her by mentioning the job, and it worked. She seemed to forget her problems with Derek for the moment, asking me questions about how I got hired and what I was going to be doing.

Before we'd even finished talking about it, other kids were arriving and things started to get busy. It looked as though the evening would go smoothly.

Then Derek came. He stood at the door, shifting from foot to foot and looking at the step.

"I wasn't sure if I was still invited or not," he said.

I didn't know either, to tell the truth. It was hard to predict how Betts would react — whether she'd be upset or glad to see him. My take on his attitude was that he was pretty glum about the breakup and might be hoping to patch things up, but that didn't guarantee how she'd feel.

"Just wait here for a sec," I told him. It took a minute to find Betts, and when I first whispered that Derek was at the door she looked happy in spite of everything that she'd said earlier. Just as quickly as her face lit up, though, she pushed it aside and scowled.

"Why don't you go talk to him," I suggested. "I didn't know whether or not I should ask him in, in case it bothered you."

"He can come in if he wants. Makes no difference to me," she sniffed, once again contradicting what she'd said earlier.

"He looks pretty unhappy," I mentioned. That seemed to cheer her, and I watched her rapidly changing expressions with amusement.

"Yeah?"

"Really. What harm can it do to talk to him for a minute?"

"I suppose ... just for a minute, though," she agreed.

Even though she sounded reluctant, I knew better. I could tell she was dying to talk to him, and I knew I'd been right when a good half hour passed before I saw either one of them again. When I did, they were holding hands and smiling from ear to ear.

Chapter Four

I was almost late on my first morning at work! You know how it is when your alarm rings and you swat it — kind of annoyed because you know it's a weekend and you don't have to get up? Then you remember that there was a reason you set it for this particular day? Well, that's what happened, and I nearly fell back to sleep before I realized what I was doing.

But anyway, I got up and got there on time after all. Lisa, the lady who'd interviewed me, led me to the kitchen and introduced me to the cook, whose name was Ben.

I don't know quite what I'd been expecting, but the guy in the kitchen sure wasn't it. He looked like he was barely in his twenties, with long hair tied back in a ponytail and earrings in his eyebrows and lip.

"Hey, Shelly." He grinned at me.

"It's Shelby, actually," I said, feeling foolish for some reason, as though it was my fault he'd gotten my name wrong.

"Well, then, *Shelby*," Ben waved a hand about the room, "welcome to my kitchen."

"Thanks." I felt awkward. It wasn't that he was saying or doing anything to make me feel that way. I suppose it was just that I was already nervous and ill at ease.

"Together, we will create magic here, no?"

It seemed a strange way to phrase a question — with the word "no" at the end.

"I believe the magic is your department," I said, trying to sound casual when in truth my stomach was all tight. "I think I'm just here to wash dishes and peel vegetables and stuff."

He laughed, throwing his head back and letting his whole body vibrate with it, as though I'd made a really funny joke. I managed to force a smile.

"So, your first job will be to cut out our lunch special," he said, once he'd gotten himself back under control. "There's a cutter there on the counter."

I picked it up and followed him to the other side of the room, where something pale was spread out over a table.

"Just cut this out. Dip the cutter in warm water if it gets sticky, though it shouldn't. The portions can go on this tray."

"What *is* this?" I asked.

"Polenta. I prepared it this morning and now it's cool enough to cut. It's served with a sauce over it." He smiled and chuckled. "Cornmeal. That's all it is. But it sounds fancy, no? Customers love to order things that sound elegant."

"They're kind of small," I commented as I lifted the first few onto the tray. Each circular shape was about as big around as a doughnut, but not as thick.

Ben laughed again and made some remark about how the less you give people to eat, the more they think they're getting the royal treatment. It didn't make sense to me, but then I'd *starve* if I had to make it from one meal to the next on the amount of food in each of these polenta servings.

When I'd finished with that, I had a whole bunch of vegetables to chop up for soup and to be served with main course dishes. It seemed as though I'd never make my way through the mountain of produce, and I started worrying that I'd get fired because the soup wouldn't be ready in time for lunch.

"Here," Ben said at one point, taking a pile of peeled carrots and laying them on a chopping board. The blade on his knife flew up and down so fast I couldn't follow its movement. They were chopped in seconds! Next, he took celery stalks that I'd trimmed and washed and did the same with them. It seemed as though my work had been reduced by twenty-five percent in less than a minute. It made me feel like a total snail.

"Before Madam Anorexia comes in and bites your head off," he said when I thanked him.

"You mean Lisa?" I asked, kind of shocked that he'd speak that way about his employer. It *did* sort of suit her, though, thin as she was.

"Yes. Only her real name is Alessia, after our grandmother. Just like my name is really Beniamino."

"After your ..." I began. "You mean, you and, uh, Lisa, are related?"

"She's my cousin. Our fathers are brothers. But don't hold it against me." He turned back to the stove, where something was simmering in a pot. "I'd like to tell you that deep down inside Lisa is really a warm and loving person. I can't, though, because I dislike lying."

At that very moment Lisa came breezing through the doorway. I felt my face grow warm and red, as though I'd been the one saying those things about her.

"Lisa," Ben said with a smirk and a little bow. "To what do we owe the pleasure of your charming presence? And how may I be of service to you?"

"You can stop the nonsense," she suggested. She turned to look at me, and past me, to the pile of vegetables behind me on the counter. Then her eyes strayed to the smaller pile still waiting to be peeled or chopped.

"You aren't finished yet."

"Very good!" Ben cried before I could answer. "Your powers of observation amaze us, one and all. Now, shoo, be off with you. I have work to do."

Lisa frowned but didn't answer him. Instead, she rolled her eyes as if to ask why she had to put up with such a moron.

"You have to work faster," she told me.

"I'll try," I said.

"There are already pots waiting to be washed," she pointed out. "You're not even finished the vegetables, and you haven't started ..."

"Because I have been giving her other tasks to do as well," Ben cut her off. "Will you please leave the kitchen matters in my hands. If Shelby doesn't work out, I'll let you know, but leave it to me to put her to use where she's most needed. Everything will get done."

Lisa looked as though she had a few things to say to him. Her mouth opened, but a sudden, strange noise in the walls distracted her.

"What's that?" I asked, startled. It sounded as though there was something trapped in there, banging and howling all at once.

"It's only the pipes." Ben's hand swept downward, dismissing my alarm. "I just turned on the water to fill the sink. It does this sometimes. Air trapped or something. Nothing to worry about."

Having been cut off for the second time, Lisa sighed in exasperation and left the kitchen. As she passed me on her way to the door, she hissed something that sounded like "Faster!" though I couldn't be certain.

Ben must have heard it too. "Don't worry," he grinned. "She never brings her whip to work. Anyway, you're doing fine."

I didn't feel as though I was doing fine, but I can say one thing about my first day on the job: it flew by faster than I could have believed possible. There was so much to do, and when the waitresses, Nadine and another, older lady named Ruth, got there, things really got busy.

I don't know how Ben kept up. Nadine and Ruth kept coming in with lunch orders written on the pads they carried in pockets of their aprons. They'd clip each order to a wheel that was hanging over the main work area, and Ben would glance at it and fly into action, while still taking care of everything else that was already on the go. It gave the illusion that he had about ten hands, all moving at once.

If I'd had as much to do as he did, I'd have been so overwhelmed I would have given up, but rather than getting flustered, he whistled and hummed as he worked. As for me, I could barely keep up with the rapidly growing piles of dishes even though all I had to do with them was load them in the dishwasher. It wasn't like the kind people have at home but rather reminded me of a car wash. Rollers slowly moved trays of dishes through the machine until they came out the other side, washed and rinsed and almost too hot to touch. I left them for a few moments before unloading and by then they were dry because any remaining water on them had steamed off.

Nadine went out of her way to be friendly to me, stopping for a few seconds now and then to offer a word or two of encouragement. The other waitress was nice too, but quieter and less inclined to chat.

By the end of my shift, I was worn out. I almost hoped Lisa would tell me I wasn't working out, but when I was getting ready to leave, she came into the kitchen, looking around carefully.

"You did okay," she said, without the slightest sign of being pleased. "Come in Tuesday, after school, and I will give you your schedule for the next few weeks."

I told her thanks, but if she heard me she didn't acknowledge it.

CHAPTER FIVE

The first few days at work were the hardest, but by the end of the second week I was getting used to the job. Most days I even finished my work with time to spare for a few extra things, like taking glasses or bread and butter plates out to the dining room, something the waitresses usually did when they had a few free moments.

We were all kept pretty busy most of the time. Between the lunch and dinner rushes I had piles of dishes, as well as whatever Ben needed done, while the waitresses had to clean and set the tables and do things like shape the big, soft cloth serviettes into cones and stand them upside down at each place setting.

And then of course there was always the odd customer who'd stop in for a meal, or even just dessert, between normal mealtimes, so the place wasn't often completely empty.

One afternoon, Nadine came into the kitchen looking a bit agitated. "If you're not busy in here," she whispered, "would you find something to do in the dining area for a few minutes?"

"Sure," I agreed. "I have some cutlery and stuff to bring out to the trays anyway. What's up?"

"It's nothing, really. Just me being overly nervous, probably. But I have this customer who kind of gives me the creeps. He comes in the middle of the afternoon some days — for coffee and pie — and he just sits there and stares at me. Normally, Lisa is around, but she's gone to do the bank deposit or something, so I'm like totally alone with him right now."

"Well, let me just get this apron off and I'll come help you set the tables up. By the time we get that done, Lisa should be back."

"I feel silly asking you to do this," she admitted. "It's not as if he's ever actually said or done anything — it's just that he's so strange, staring but never saying a word."

"It's no problem," I assured her. Ben waved me away when I went to explain to him that I was going to the other room with Nadine for a bit.

"My dear cousin may care *desperately* what you do every moment that you're here," he laughed, "but I am the sane one in the family, remember?"

I could see right away what Nadine meant about the guy in the dining room. It was definitely a bit weird, the way he sat there, his eyes following her under big, bushy eyebrows. He watched every step she took. I wondered if he was from Little River or not, since I couldn't remember ever seeing him before. Of course, I don't know everyone in town.

Lisa was a while getting back that day, but it didn't matter. The guy finished his pie and coffee, dropped some change on the table, and got up to leave.

"Come with me," Nadine said, talking through clenched teeth, her voice low.

I went along, even though I felt a bit foolish accompanying her to the cash register. It was good that I did, though, because she was so flustered that she couldn't get the cash register to work. It won't operate until you put in a key and turn it, but Nadine forgot about that and tried to ring in his purchase without the key until I reminded her.

"Thank goodness you were here!" she declared after he'd taken his change and gone silently out the door. "I was so rattled I'd never have remembered the key. As it was, I could hardly remember which one to use."

"What are all the others for?" I asked, noticing how full the ring was.

"I dunno. Probably for the entrance doors and stuff they keep locked in the office."

"If they ever lose this key ring they're sunk then," I said, "though maybe they have a copy."

"Yeah. Probably. Anyway, thanks again. I don't know what I would have done without you." Impulsively, Nadine leaned forward and gave me a quick hug.

"Hey, it was nothing. I like getting out of the kitchen once in a while," I assured her.

"You don't like your job?" she asked.

"It's not that," I said. "It's just that, well, I feel a tiny bit uncomfortable around Ben sometimes. I feel almost silly mentioning it. It's not like some huge problem or anything. But he's kind of flirtatious, if you know what I mean."

"I know *exactly* what you mean," she said, nodding. "He's the same way with me. My boyfriend, Leo, gets ticked off about it too, but I think it's harmless enough. I don't think Ben really means anything by it."

"Well, just tell your boyfriend that he acts that way with everyone," I suggested. I couldn't imagine Greg getting upset over something like that, when it wasn't even my fault.

She sighed. "To tell you the truth, Shelby, I've been kind of wanting to break up with Leo for a while now. I just don't like the thought of the hassle."

"Really? How come?" I asked — just before I realized that it was none of my business. I was getting as bad as my gossip-loving friend Betts!

"It's not only that he's a bit jealous and possessive," she said, "he's full of himself too. He works out almost every day, and he's fanatical about what he eats and drinks." She smiled ruefully. "A girl likes to think her boyfriend cares about her, but if Leo loves anyone, it's himself." Her voice lowered to a whisper. "He even looks at himself every chance he gets, if you know what I mean."

"Like walking by a window where he can see his reflection, and that sort of thing?" I knew a few girls who did that too. It always amazed me that they seemed to think they were doing it on the sly, as if no one else could see what they were up to.

"Exactly. He's so arrogant! He acts like I should be, I dunno, thankful, I guess, that he's going out with me. Like I won the big prize and I should appreciate him more." She shuddered as she talked about him, which is hardly ever a good sign in a relationship.

I was getting a fairly good picture of this Leo person. He didn't sound exactly charming, but then not all guys can be like Greg.

"He's kind of controlling too," she went on. It seemed she really wanted to talk some of this stuff out, so I just listened and nodded every so often to show I was paying attention. It seemed as though she was pretty fed up with the guy.

"He's on my case about *something* all the time. I don't get enough exercise. I shouldn't drink pop or eat junk food. He hates it when I have a Pepsi — and all I ever drink is the diet stuff! I can't imagine what he'd do if it was regular pop. All Leo wants to do is work out at the gym and admire his muscles. I think he'd like it if I was a female bodybuilder or something."

"So he's pretty strong then?"

"I guess. Anyway, none of this is your problem. I'm sorry I brought it all up, because he's not really a bad guy, and I'm making him sound horrible. I guess it's just that he's wrong for me, and I've come to the place where I realize I need to end things, but I really don't want to hurt him."

I've never had to break up with anyone, though I've seen Betts do it a few times. Well, I haven't actually *seen* her do it, but you know what I mean. I always felt sorry for the guys. It must be awful to be dating someone and all of a sudden they decide they don't like you anymore, or you bug them in some way, or whatever other excuse you get handed when you get dumped.

"Well, it's usually best to just go ahead and get it over with," I said, like I was offering advice from the vast wealth of my own experiences.

"I know," she sighed. "Anyway, I'd better get back to work. I have to change the dinner specials in the menus or Lisa will wonder what I've been doing the whole time she was gone."

CHAPTER SIX

The next Saturday was one of my days off, and I was eager to do something that didn't involve scrubbing or peeling. Mainly, I wanted to do something *outside*, so I was excited when Betts and Derek and Greg and I made plans for an afternoon hike.

Greg got the loan of his dad's car and we went to Catbird Cove, a place with really cool walking trails. There are even a couple of places where rope bridges hang suspended high over streams that pulse through deep, wide crevices in the land.

I've never been afraid of that sort of thing, but Betts is a bit nervous of heights. Actually, that's putting it pretty mildly. Terrified would be a more accurate description. She can't even look over the balcony from the second floor without getting woozy!

I don't quite understand her fear, but I sure don't

make fun of it. When I was a little girl, I was scared of anyone wearing a toque with a face in it. You know the kind, where you can just see the eyes and mouth. Anyway, any time someone happened along with one of those on, I'd just totally freak — screeching and crying like you wouldn't believe. I can remember not being able to catch my breath because I was so upset.

It seems ridiculous looking back. I mean, it's not like my parents didn't explain that they were just people with hats on. Once, trying to help, my dad even put one on in a department store. He did it real slow, talking to me as he slid it down over his face, telling me that it was okay, it was just Daddy. Even so, the second his face disappeared under the mask I nearly hollered my lungs out. People around us were probably thinking he was doing something mean to me, the way I carried on!

The thing is, even at that age, I'm pretty sure I *understood* that it was just a hat. Knowing that didn't seem to matter — there was something about the sight of it that got my heart pounding like crazy. I couldn't be talked out of it, and it wasn't until I got older that I stopped being nervous of that kind of toque.

I don't know much about phobias, so I don't know if that's what I had, but I'm almost certain that Betts's fear of heights is a phobia. Luckily, Derek isn't the type to try to force her to overcome it, like some guys might do. He's pretty patient and understanding of the whole thing.

So, anyway, like I was saying, we were at Catbird Cove and we wanted to climb over one of the rope bridges to get to Swallow Peak, which has an awesome view of a waterfall. Or, actually, three of us wanted to. Betts wasn't what you could call keen on the idea. Still, after taking a few moments to build up her courage, she said she thought she could do it.

It started out okay, her holding onto Derek's hand and looking straight ahead.

"Don't look down," Derek said in a soothing voice. "You're doing great. Just don't look down."

Betts looked down. And, of course, the second she did, she shrieked and panicked. That wasn't good, because she let go of the rope railing and grabbed Derek, which threw his balance off and made the whole thing sway like crazy. That did nothing to calm Betts, who started crying and screaming all at once.

Greg and I were a few feet behind them, and I can tell you, it's a horrible sight to see someone in that kind of panic. Her face was twisted in terror, and the more frightened she got, the more she thrashed around. This caused the bridge to move wildly, which just increased her fear.

Derek looked pretty scared himself, by that point. I guess I shouldn't blame him for what he did next, and maybe it was for the best because if Betts had kept on, she might have ended up capsizing the whole thing. Still, it seemed kind of cowardly and selfish.

What he did was wrench himself away from her and take off to the other side. Betts immediately dropped to her knees and then flattened out against the floor of the bridge, which is made of slats of wood roped together. Her screeches turned into low sobs and moans as she clung to the edges with white-knuckled hands.

"Betts?" I said tentatively, hoping to calm her. "It's okay. We're coming to get you."

"I can't let go," she yelled angrily, though no one had suggested she should.

"No need to," Greg said softly as we inched toward her, moving slowly so as not to make the bridge sway anymore. "You can hold on as tight as you need. No one will make you let go."

"Well, I *have to get out of here*," she yelled, as though he'd been encouraging her to spend the next few years there.

"Are you okay, Betts?" Derek called from the other side.

I managed to keep from saying anything nasty to him, even though he'd abandoned her right in the middle of her panic attack and I was pretty ticked off about it.

Betts didn't answer either, though I'm not sure if she even heard him. Mostly, she was concentrating on holding on as tight as she could.

It was Greg who answered. "She's fine," he said with a calm assurance that would have fooled anyone who wasn't watching. "We're going to get her back on solid ground. Stay where you are until then."

"I think I'm going to throw up," Betts said. She was shaking and very pale.

"Betts," Greg said, still speaking in an even, calm voice, "close your eyes and take a deep breath through your nose. Then tell me what you smell."

At first she didn't do what he was asking, but after a few moments, with him repeating it slowly and softly, she actually went ahead and did it.

"Now, what do you smell?" he asked, before she'd even fully exhaled.

"Trees, I guess. Why?"

"Trees. Good. I think there are other things too, but we'll get to that in a minute," he said, kneeling as he spoke. "I'm almost to you now, Betts, so if you feel something touch your hand, it's just going to be me. Is it okay if I put my hand on yours?"

"Yeah, it's okay." Her voice was still tremulous, but a little less panicked than it had been a few moments before.

"Now, getting back to the trees and stuff, I want you to concentrate really hard and see how many things you can identify only by smell. No peeking." He'd reached her by this point, and I hung back just a little as he slid his hand over hers.

"I smell water, and flowers, probably," Betts said. It was clear that she knew what was going on — that he was distracting her — and she seemed determined to force herself to go along. I suppose anything that kept her from thinking about the situation she was in was more than welcome to her.

"Good, good. Can you take my hand, Betts?"

"I don't think so." She clutched harder at the edge of the walkway as though to prove that she was telling the truth.

"Okay, that's okay," he said quietly. Then he talked to her for what seemed ages, not about her present predicament, but about things like movies and music and stuff like that. Just as he'd done by getting her to identify smells, distracting her seemed to relax her a little. Once she was a bit calmer, he persuaded her to slide her hand forward just a few inches, without actually letting go of anything, and then to move herself forward as well.

With incredible patience, Greg talked her through move after move like that. Each one would only mean an inch or two gained toward getting her off the bridge, and it took hours before she finally reached the end.

Betts's lip began to tremble when she saw that solid ground was right ahead of her. She allowed Greg and me to each take a hand and help her as she rose, first to her knees and then upright once she'd come forward enough to stand on the ground.

Derek crossed back over to our side then, looking sheepish. He apologized over and over, but Betts didn't seem to be in the mood to talk about it, at least not to *him*. She just shrugged him off and hardly spoke to him for the rest of the afternoon.

Once she was completely recovered from her ordeal, we stuck to footpaths through the forest and along several of the brooks that wound through the area.

Derek was trying very hard to please Betts, who was barely responding to anything he said or did. I couldn't help thinking it was a shame to see a nice afternoon turned into a source of trouble between them. After their recent breakup and all, it looked as though their relationship was on pretty shaky ground, and I wondered if they were going to last the summer.

CHAPTER SEVEN

"Shelby! I need you to do something for me."

I still wasn't quite used to the way Lisa spoke to me, like some kind of drill sergeant barking orders. It was so completely different from the way she talked to customers, when her voice was all silky and pleasant to an extreme.

"Yes?" I asked, keeping my voice polite even though I felt like asking if it would kill her to speak to me like I was a human being.

"Go to Nadine's apartment and tell her I just got a large reservation and I need another girl. See if she can work tonight."

"You can't phone her?"

"If I could phone her, I wouldn't ask you to go, would I?" Lisa said shortly. "She just moved to a new place and her phone is not yet hooked up. Here is the address. Go quickly. It's raining a little, so take this umbrella."

I took the umbrella and slip of paper, both of which she thrust toward me as though she were angry, and started toward the door, remembering at the last moment that I was still wearing an apron. I took it off and tossed it over the just-emptied dishwasher then hurried out the side entrance that employees used.

It was nice to get out of the steamy kitchen for a few minutes, and I took a deep breath of fresh air as I headed toward the street. I love the smell outside when it's raining, and a citrus scent also hung in the air, which surprised me a little. I wondered if Ben was cooking something with oranges. It seemed unlikely, since our daily special had been Duck à l'Orange just a few days before.

The address Lisa had given me was only a few blocks away, near the old post office. It was a big old building that hadn't been very well maintained, at least on the outside. The paint was faded and peeling and the roof looked kind of scabby, as if the shingles were curling up around the edges. It looked pretty dismal, but I closed my umbrella and hurried up the steps and into the entryway.

The inside was no improvement, at least in the hallway and wide, open stairwell. A bare bulb hung there, offering the only source of light — which might have been just as well, considering the uncared-for look of the place. Even though it was dimly lit, I could see that little attention had been given to cleaning, and the walls were cracked and chipped in places, probably from being banged with furniture when tenants were moving in or out.

The address Lisa had written out for me said that Nadine lived in apartment E, but I couldn't see any letters on any of the four doors in the downstairs hall. Before I could think about how to find her, a creak to my right told me one of the doors was opening.

"Mary? Is it you then?" a voice as creaky as the door inquired. "I've been expecting you."

"Oh, I'm not …" I began.

"Where's your bag?" She peered about the floor, then at my face. "You don't look like Mary Poppins," she accused. "Let's see you work that thing."

She pointed at the umbrella as she made her last remark. I hardly knew how to react, I was so startled. I stammered something about not being Mary Poppins, which isn't the sort of thing I often have to deny to anyone. She looked dreadfully displeased at the news.

"I'm just looking for Nadine — a girl I work with," I added, as though that explained why I'd disappointed her in not being able to open my umbrella and float up into the air.

"Oh, that one," the odd little creature muttered. "She's upstairs, right above me."

"Well, thank you very much," I said, though it seemed doubtful to say the least that she might know what she was talking about. Since I had no other leads, I decided to go ahead and check, just in case. Besides, knocking on doors seemed the only way I was likely to find her, and that seemed as good a starting place as any.

I was surprised when Nadine opened the door a moment after I'd knocked.

"Hey, Shelby, what's up?"

I explained that Lisa had sent me to ask her about working that evening. She agreed right away to come in.

"Extra hours would be great," she said. "I need to get paint and stuff to fix this place up a bit. It's not as bad as you'd think from the rest of the building, though. Come see."

She beckoned me into the apartment, and I could see right away that it really *wasn't* that bad inside. She had a kitchen, living room, bedroom, and bathroom. The rooms were large, with big windows, and they seemed to have been cared for fairly well.

"I could have gotten an apartment in a better building," she said, "but the rooms here are so much bigger than most places. I like the space, and I think a bit of paint and some new curtains will improve this a lot."

"Your landlord won't pay for paint?" I asked.

"Land*lady*, and she's crazier than the birds. No point asking her for anything." I realized she was talking about the odd woman I'd met downstairs.

"That was the *landlady*?"

"Oh, did you meet her?" Nadine giggled. "When I came to see about the apartment, she sang me some song about being sixteen going on seventeen when she showed it to me. And she tried to do a dance at the same time, but that didn't work out so well. She nearly tripped over her own feet."

"Goodness!"

"Yeah. It's a wonder she can keep it together enough to collect rent and stuff. I think she's supposed to keep the place clean too, but I haven't seen any sign that she pays much attention to that. A couple who live down the hall here told me she's an aunt to the owner, and he kind of lets her do the job out of sympathy and on account of she has nowhere else to go."

"Well, that's nice of him, I guess," I said doubtfully, "but you'd think they'd lose a lot of potential tenants when people show up to ask about a place and she says crazy things or does some strange performance or whatever."

"True. The couple told me that she's *obsessed* with Julie Andrews movies."

"That explains her thinking I was Mary Poppins," I said, feeling rather sorry for the poor old thing. "Still, when I mentioned you, she directed me to this apartment right away. She must be a little lucid."

"A very little," Nadine laughed. "Anyway, I didn't mean to keep you this long. Lisa will be having a fit."

I said goodbye then and hurried back to The Steak Place, told Lisa that Nadine would be able to come in as she'd asked, and returned to the kitchen.

Ben was stirring a pot of sauce, which a quick peek told me was for pasta. Remembering that I'd smelled oranges earlier, I started to ask him what he was making with them in it. My words were drowned out by the sudden clanging and moaning in the water pipes.

It still startled me every time that happened. Distracted, I forgot my question and got back to work. The dishes I'd done before I went out were still stacked and waiting to be taken to the dining room. I carried trays of them out there and put them in place. Sue, the waitress who was on that afternoon, was in the middle of her lunch, but she still jumped up and offered to help me put them away.

"Don't be silly," I said. "Eat while you have a chance. The place won't stay empty for long."

As if my words had drawn him, the fellow who'd been staring at Nadine the other day came wandering in. He ordered pie and coffee, but this time he ate with his head down, completely uninterested in watching the waitress.

CHAPTER EIGHT

"Hey, do you guys want to do a good deed?"

"Good deeds are the very reason I rise in the morning," Greg said, getting up from his seat so he could make a silly little bow. "I would but there were more opportunities to perform acts of kindness for my fellow man."

"I'll put you down as a 'yes' then," I giggled. It delights me when Greg talks all formal and serious that way, which is a habit of his that I didn't always find so endearing.

"When?" Derek asked.

"What is it?" Betts wanted to know.

The four of us were at The Scream Machine on a Thursday evening, and I'd been waiting for just the right moment to ask. Betts and Derek seemed to be getting along okay today, but from recent experience I knew that could change at any moment. Laughter could turn into bickering at the most unexpected times, and it seemed that Greg and I had to become peace-keepers all too often. Their problems made me appreciate my relationship with Greg even more.

Anyway, everything was calm and peaceful right then, so I plunged in.

"There's a girl I work with, Nadine Gardiner," I began. "She's just a few years older than us, but she's on her own. She could use some help this weekend. Even a few hours would be great."

"Doing what?" Betts asked.

"Count me in," Greg said, "if it can be on Saturday. I work Friday evening and all day Sunday."

"She just moved into a new apartment and she's going to paint it." I answered Betts's question first. "Saturday would be perfect. She and I both work, but not until four o'clock, so if we got an early start, we could get a lot done by mid-afternoon."

"I don't know how to paint," Betts said.

"Me neither, never did it before," Derek agreed.

"How hard can it be?" I asked. "You just push a roller up and down the wall."

"So, what if it's all streaky and stuff?"

"I imagine you could just go over it again with more paint. C'mon, guys. She's got no one to give her a hand with it. Her boyfriend won't even help because he says it's too unhealthy to breathe in paint fumes and besides he has a noon appointment with his trainer."

"Sounds like a nice guy," Greg commented, shaking his head.

"Oh, he's a real catch. Jealous, bossy, and all wrapped up in himself. Actually, Nadine's planning to dump him. I don't really know him, though I've seen him in the restaurant a few times, but from what she's told me, he's a total jerk."

"Typical guy, then," Betts observed unfairly.

I took a deep breath, thinking her remark would quickly turn into a fight between her and Derek. It would be hard to stay neutral if it did, seeing as how she seemed to be deliberately *looking* for an argument. It didn't happen, though. Derek ignored what she'd said and agreed to come and help at Nadine's place.

Then Betts said she'd come as well, and it was all settled. We'd meet at my house and all go over together.

By the time Saturday morning came, Greg and I had gathered up some trays and rollers and brushes from our dads. We figured we had enough stuff for everyone to be doing something productive at the same time.

"We're ready," I called out to Dad. He'd promised to drive us over and pick us up at three so I'd still have time to shower and change for work.

"I have a couple of things to do around town later," he told us as he dropped us off about ten minutes later.

"Which apartment is it? I'll bring a party pizza by around noon."

I told him how to find her apartment and hugged him good and hard because he deserved it. Then the four of us trooped up the stairs and knocked on Nadine's door.

"Shelby!" she said, surprised to see me there with a group of friends. "Oh, goodness. I'm sorry, but I can't invite you in today. I'm painting my place and everything's in a big mess. I think I mentioned that I was going to be doing that, but I guess you forgot."

"I didn't forget," I said. "We're all here to help you paint. This is Betts and her boyfriend, Derek, and this is my boyfriend, Greg. Everyone, this is Nadine."

She looked stunned and delighted all at once, inviting us in and murmuring that she couldn't believe it and thanking us over and over.

"I'm just here because I figure it will look good on my resumé," Greg said, smiling. "Which room do you want to start in?"

"I'd like to get the kitchen done first, since it's the first room people see when they come in. Then, if we have time, the living room next."

"Okay, Derek, let's you and I move the table and chairs and stuff into the other room so we can get started."

He and Derek each grabbed an end of the table and disappeared around the corner with it.

"Where's your bathroom?" Betts asked. "My mom made me bring some old things to wear while I'm painting, but I'll have to change into them here. There was no way I was wearing them on the street."

Nadine showed her where the bathroom was and then came back. "This is so awesome of you guys," she said.

"None of us were busy today, and I knew you weren't getting any help from Leo," I said, setting down the trays I'd been holding.

"That's all over," she said, giving me a nod as though I'd asked something else at the same time and she was answering it. "I'm through with him."

"Seriously? You broke up with Leo?"

"Yup. The other day. I just couldn't take any more of his self-centredness, or his telling me what to do all the time. So I told him I didn't want to see him anymore."

"How'd he take it?"

She rolled her eyes. "I think he was in shock, actually. Like, totally unable to believe that anyone would dump a prize like him. He kind of stormed off in a state of disbelief, but he hasn't called me since so I guess he's accepted it.

"Anyway, I couldn't afford to buy mirrors for every room in my apartment, and Leo could never be truly happy without them," she added with a giggle.

"So, you're sure he's not going to freak out or anything?"

"I can't see it. Leo is too proud to make a scene."

I hoped she was right.

Betts returned then, looking cute as could be in a big blue shirt that must have belonged to her dad at one point in time. The flaps hung down almost to her knees, and she had to roll the sleeves up a couple of turns in order for her hands to be visible at all.

"I feel ridiculous," she said.

"But you *look* adorable," Derek assured her. I was glad to see that they were getting along so well at the moment. It wouldn't be much fun working together if they were at each other's throats.

Nadine looked at the cans of paint and checked them against the colour code cards she'd brought from the paint store. She pulled out the one for the kitchen, and before long we were all working away. We decided that the girls would do the edges where the paint had to be applied with brushes, and the guys would roll the rest of the walls.

It only took a little over an hour to have the whole kitchen done, and we'd finished the living room too by the time Dad got there with pizza, juice, and bottles of water.

"This is the most amazing thing that's ever happened to me in my life," Nadine said after Dad had dropped off our lunch.

"Hey, it's fun," Betts remarked, and I could see that she meant it. It was true too. While we'd worked steadily, there'd been a lot of joking and laughter the whole time. Betts isn't what you'd call used to doing much in the line of work, coming from a fairly well-off family that employs a cleaning lady. She doesn't even have to keep her own room tidy.

Not that she's spoiled — or, at least, she doesn't *act* spoiled. When she's at my place and it's my turn for dishes or whatever, she always helps out. So, it's not like she's got some kind of "I'm a princess" attitude. It's just that she normally doesn't have to do anything.

I thought we'd get all the rooms done that day, but it turned out that after we'd eaten lunch we got kind of lazy and worked sluggishly the rest of the time we were there. Still, all that was left when we cleaned up for the day was the bathroom, and it was too small for all of us to work in at once anyway.

Nadine thanked us again and promised that she was going to invite us all over for a party one night the next weekend.

Of course, she didn't know what was coming.

CHAPTER NINE

When I got to work that evening I saw that Ben wasn't in the kitchen. Instead, it was the second cook, a crabby middle-aged woman who'd haughtily introduced herself to me the first time I'd worked under her as Mrs. Something-or-other — a long name that my brain hadn't taken in.

I'd heard Lisa call her Carlotta, but her attitude toward me didn't invite familiarity so I just called her "ma'am" to her face, which seemed okay with her.

She took her role as my supervisor very seriously and liked to make sure that I was busy at all times. I'd already learned not to rush when I was doing anything on her shifts, since she'd just pile on more and more work. Not that I didn't expect to work hard, but this woman was a slave-driver! I hardly had time to breathe between the orders she barked out, sometimes accompanied by insults. Even Lisa looked positively easygoing next to her.

Unfortunately, that Saturday wasn't a busy evening in the restaurant. That meant there was spare time — or, I should say, there *would* have been spare time. Not with Carlotta in charge of me. She got the brainwave that I should lug up the supplies that had been delivered the day before. The place had been in the middle of a lunch rush when the delivery guy came in with the order, and Lisa had impatiently told him to put the piles of boxes downstairs for the time being. There was no way anyone could stop what they were doing to put stuff away right then.

"You, girl!" Carlotta kind of yelled, her usual way of getting my attention. "You need job to do; you bring up boxes from basement. Put away."

Her English wasn't great, but it was never a problem for her to make her orders understood! I could hardly believe that she expected me to do that all by myself.

"Uh, Ben said he and I would do that together on his next shift," I said, knowing full well it wasn't going to change her mind. I'd seen the delivery guy strain when he was carrying some of the boxes, though, and dreaded the thought of having to wrestle them upstairs all by myself.

"What? You want paid to do nothing? You want maybe we should just give you money to stay home?"

"That's not what I meant."

"Go then! Do like I tell you!"

I trudged downstairs and surveyed the piles of boxes lined up along the far wall. There must have been fifty of them, and I knew a big percentage held canned goods like tomatoes and stuff.

Well, there was no sense in standing there feeling discouraged. I went over and scanned the labels that were exposed, looking for the lighter things like pasta and paper products. Maybe by the time I'd hauled the things that weren't too heavy upstairs and put them away, we'd get busy with customers and I wouldn't have time for the rest.

No such luck. It remained quiet in the place, and there was no way I could work slowly when I was unpacking stuff. Not with the dictator standing over me.

By the time I'd brought up everything that wasn't too hard to carry, I was dreading what remained downstairs. I began to wish I'd staggered them so there'd at least be a break in hauling up the weighty things. Besides, I was already getting tired from the trips up and down the stairs, and I realized I'd probably made a big mistake leaving the worst for last. It wasn't the only mistake I made either, as was pointed out in a hurry.

"Stupid girl," Carlotta said, as though it was perfectly normal to call someone you're working with names. "Why we want this in kitchen?"

I looked at the box she was referring to. Citrus air freshener.

"Where does it go?" I asked wearily.

"Is for keep place smelling nice. Not food to eat!" she snapped, as though I were a complete moron who needed that explained. "Put back."

I was angry that she'd expected me to know where it was stored without being told, but at least now I knew why I could often smell oranges around the side door. It was air freshener. I lugged it back downstairs and started bringing up the canned goods.

What really annoyed me about the whole thing wasn't even the hard work. It was the fact that Carlotta just sat back on her chair and issued orders. She never so much as lifted a finger to help. She could at least have helped me put a few things away, but no, that would be lowering herself to her assistant's level, which would never do.

It felt as though my back was breaking by the time I'd dragged the last box up and unpacked it. My arms were so sore I could hardly move them.

The only good thing was that my shift at work flew by that night. I've noticed that the busier I am doing something, the faster the time goes by. I hoped that it had dragged horribly for Carlotta!

I'd been so busy that I hadn't had time to chat with Nadine at all through the evening. It had been my intention to talk to her a bit more about the breakup with Leo, especially after I'd noticed partway through the evening that her mood had changed. I wondered if he'd dropped by and said something to her. Earlier, she'd been in perfectly good cheer, but later she looked kind of upset and almost frightened.

My shift ended an hour before hers that night. If it hadn't, when Dad arrived to take me home after work we'd have given her a ride too, and I could have asked her if there was a problem. Instead, I just said goodnight to her, aching and tired and looking forward to showering and collapsing into my bed.

Well, I thought as I climbed into the car, *I can always ask her what happened when I see her at work on Monday*. I was scheduled for a day shift and she didn't come in until four in the afternoon, but we should still have a few minutes to talk. Mondays aren't normally that busy.

It didn't work out that way, though. On Monday, when four o'clock came, one of the other waitresses showed up instead.

"Is Nadine sick?" I asked Ben. "She was supposed to work tonight."

"Nadine? No, she quit."

"Quit?" I asked, stunned. "That's impossible!"

He smiled. "This may shock you, but waitresses quit their jobs all the time. It's really not that uncommon."

"But she just moved into a new place."

"So?" His eyebrows arched with amusement as he spoke. It was obvious that he thought I was making a big deal out of nothing, and I started to feel a bit foolish.

"Well, she has to pay the rent and stuff. Why would she quit her job?"

"Maybe she found another job." He shrugged. "How do I know *why*? I just know she called Lisa yesterday and said she quit."

I went to Lisa and asked her what, exactly, Nadine had said.

"How would I remember?" She seemed as uninterested in the subject as Ben had been. "All I know is she didn't give notice. Very thoughtless. Now I have no one to fill her shifts and I have to find someone else right away."

"Did her voice sound funny or anything when she called?" I asked, concern growing in me.

Lisa seemed to have run out of patience. "The girl quit, that's all I know. I can't stand here all day talking about it. And I would think that *you* might have work to do."

Discouraged, I went back to work, glad that my shift would be over at six. I decided to stop by Nadine's place later, to find out what was going on, but when I got home I was met with some unexpected news.

"Shelby," Mom said, putting her arms around me, "I'm afraid I have something sad to tell you. Your Great-Aunt Isabel passed away this evening."

CHAPTER TEN

You can hardly blame me for forgetting about Nadine for the next two days. My great-aunt's death pretty much took over centre stage as far as my family was concerned. There was the wake and the funeral, besides which we had relatives from out of town at our place for most of the meals during the whole thing.

My mom cried a lot, which made me sad. Well, actually, the truth is I felt pretty sad anyway. That was a surprise because I'd never been overly fond of Great-Aunt Isabel.

She'd had a lot of habits and mannerisms that I'd found silly and annoying, but they suddenly didn't appear to me in the same light at all. Instead, I could picture things that she might have said or done, and instead of bothersome, they seemed sad and pathetic.

In a room full of people, Great-Aunt Isabel had liked to be the one who was talking. More accurately, she'd liked to be the one being listened to. She often put me in mind of Lady Catherine de Bourgh — a character from *Pride and Prejudice* — except Great-Aunt Isabel, unlike that other rather self-centred lady, had neither power nor wealth.

It was like she'd longed to be important somehow, as though her whole worth was tied up in what other people thought of her. In the end, none of that mattered, and the only thing that seemed to be left was memories of an old woman who'd had a great need to hold the interest and attention of those around her. In fact, there'd been little about her that would command much notice from anyone.

So it was totally unexpected that standing there, looking at her lying all still and silent in that coffin, a huge flood of belated affection came rushing over me. It made me feel just awful, thinking of how I'd disliked going to her place for visits and how I'd secretly made fun of her, even if it was just to myself.

I'd never stopped, not once, to wonder about her life — what it was like and whether or not she might be lonely or sad. Strangely, as soon as her life was over, that seemed to be the only thing I could think for the next few days. Finally, I couldn't stand it anymore.

"Do you think your Great-Aunt Isabel was happy?" I asked Mom when we were on our way home from the last wake session. I don't know what I expected her to say. I think I was really looking for something to soothe my feelings of guilt. Like, if Isabel had been happy all her life, it didn't matter if my attitude toward her had been less than loving.

"Happy?" Mom pondered before answering. When she did, she spoke slowly and thoughtfully, like she was telling the answer to herself at the same time. "Why, I suppose she had happy *and* sad moments, like the rest of us."

Her reply didn't exactly satisfy me, but I couldn't seem to find the words to ask anything else that would tell me what I wanted to know. Or maybe, right then, I realized I didn't actually want to know how Isabel had lived and what her life had been like. It might be best to put such thoughts out of my head altogether.

The funeral was the next morning, and once that was over with and she'd disappeared into the ground, it seemed as though Isabel's whole existence had been pointless. She and her husband, who'd died years and years earlier, hadn't had any children, so there was no one to carry on in her place, if that's even what kids do when their parents are gone.

Greg and his dad, Dr. Taylor, were parked in front of our house when we got home from the graveyard.

They'd been at both the funeral and the short burial ceremony, but had left before we did.

Greg took my hand and squeezed it. We walked silently into the house, behind my folks and his dad, who were talking quietly.

They'd brought lunch, a big container of home-made soup, along with rolls and raspberry pie. I set the table while the soup warmed on the stove, the smell of it making my stomach growl, though I hadn't known I was hungry. Dr. Taylor is a psychologist, but he's also a fantastic cook.

He and Greg moved here to Little River last summer after Mrs. Taylor died in a fire. Since then, Dr. Taylor has been working on a book, which my mom says is helping him heal from his grief. As I put the last few things on the table I wondered if this whole funeral thing today had brought back a lot of sad memories for him and Greg.

I didn't like to ask Greg that, but as we ate, it struck me that the conversation around the table seemed perfectly normal. In fact, you'd never have guessed that we were all gathered after someone's death, or that anyone there was grieving.

Afterward, Greg and I cleaned up while our folks visited in the living room. I was wiping off the counter when he asked a question that stopped me in mid-swipe.

"How'd your friend Nadine make out with the rest of her painting? Did she get the bathroom done?"

I whirled around, startling him.

"Greg! I'd forgotten all about her," I exclaimed. "Just before all this happened, Nadine quit her job at The Steak Place."

"Oh, yeah?"

"It's very strange, though. We worked together on Saturday night, you know, the same day we painted her place, and then all of a sudden the very next day she quit."

"Maybe she found a better job."

"That's what Ben said, but I don't know. It doesn't *feel* right. Besides, don't you think she'd have mentioned it if she was looking for work somewhere else? She and I have talked quite a lot since I started working at The Steak Place. Why, she told me about her family and growing up without a dad and her mom's new husband and all kinds of things. I feel sure if she was looking for another job she'd have said something about it. But she didn't. Not a word. I have a bad feeling about the whole thing."

"You sure you're not dreaming this up — inventing something that needs detecting?" Greg leaned forward and kissed my cheek. "I think you're getting addicted to chasing clues."

"C'mon, Greg. I'm serious about this. I'm kind of worried."

"Well, why don't you just give her a call and see what's up?" Greg didn't seem any more concerned than

Ben or Lisa had been, and it made me wonder if I was overreacting. I've been known to do that.

"I can't call her," I said. "She has no phone."

"So then, drop by." He slid an arm around me. That Greg can sure be distracting sometimes! "If it's bothering you, and it seems that it is, then you should check it out and put your mind at rest."

"Yeah, that's what I'll do." Just deciding on a course of action made me feel a bit better. No doubt I'd get to her place and she'd laugh at me for being a big worrier for nothing.

I was scheduled to work at noon the next day, so first thing in the morning I took Greg's advice and walked over to Nadine's apartment. When I got to her door, a strange shiver ran up my back and I had to talk to myself about not being so dramatic and paranoid.

Except, maybe I wasn't. Maybe what I'd felt was some sort of premonition. Because when I knocked, the door swung open on its own, the slow creak of the tired old hinge almost making me scream.

I called out Nadine's name a few times, but the only reply was an ominous silence.

CHAPTER ELEVEN

I hesitated in the doorway for a few seconds and then stepped into Nadine's apartment. It probably wasn't right, just walking in like that, but it was obvious something was amiss. She'd once told me how careful she was about keeping her place bolted, and here it was with the door not even properly closed, never mind locked.

"Nadine?" I called again, moving slowly through the kitchen. I knew, deep inside, that she wasn't going to answer. My instincts had been right — something was dreadfully wrong. I looked around carefully, as though there might be some evidence that would explain why Nadine had gone off and left her place open.

On the kitchen counter sat a bowl with a half-eaten orange resting on top of peelings. Beside it were an empty coffee mug and a plate with toast crumbs. It seemed to be the remains of breakfast, but there was no way of knowing when it had been left there.

I stood for a moment, just looking around the room, as if it might offer some clue to Nadine's whereabouts. It was really quiet in there, which kind of creeped me out. I don't know what I'd been expecting, but the silence of the place was unnerving.

When I reached the living room the first thing that caught my eye was a dark, wet-looking blotch on the floor. At the sight of it, the urge to turn around and run back out the door almost overcame me. I grabbed the doorway to steady myself.

"Please tell me that isn't blood," I found myself whispering to the empty room.

Not surprisingly, the room had no comment. If I was going to find out what it was, I'd have to examine it, like you see detectives do in the movies. Of course most of that stuff is figured out by forensics these days, but I didn't happen to have a lab at home.

My legs seemed to have turned wooden and it was all I could do to make them move forward. They were shaking so hard by the time I reached the spot that sinking to my knees was no problem at all.

I leaned forward to get a closer look, which told me nothing. Reluctantly, I stuck my finger out and touched it. It was still sticky. Slowly, I raised my finger to my nose and sniffed, not even sure if I'd recognize the smell of drying blood — if in fact that's what it was. The scent was sweet and familiar, but even so it took me a few seconds to identify it.

"Pop! It's just pop." I found myself laughing nervously. "Great detecting, Shelby. You've solved the mystery of the missing cola."

Rising again, I found myself even less composed than I had been a moment before.

No doubt I was weak with relief after the scare of thinking I'd discovered a pool of blood. I made my way shakily through the rest of the apartment, being as careful as possible not to disturb anything — just in case the police ever got involved and had to check the place out. I wondered uneasily if being in there could get me charged with compromising an investigation or something.

It occurred to me then that when I'd touched the spilled pop, I'd also left my fingerprint. I was tempted to wash it up, but in the end I left it as it was. After all, it would be better to explain how my print got there than to justify deliberately tampering with anything in the apartment, even if it was something that likely wasn't one bit important. Changing anything would look a lot more suspicious.

I finished a cursory examination of the place, satisfying myself that Nadine was nowhere inside. I even opened the closets and looked under the bed, though I can't quite describe the terror I felt at the thought that

I might actually find something. I was careful, as I checked through the place, not to touch anything else with my bare hands. Instead, I took a facecloth that was hanging in the bathroom and used it over doorknobs and anything else I touched.

A light coating of dust lay completely undisturbed on the furniture, and the sink and bathtub in the bathroom were dry as a bone. Those things alone suggested no one had been there for a few days, but the fact that the paint trays we'd washed out and left to dry were still all lying on the bathroom floor clinched it for me. No one would have left them there since Saturday. It was too awkward stepping around them. Nadine would surely have moved them before now, if she'd been there.

"She hasn't been here since Saturday?" I found myself asking aloud. That didn't quite fit either. What about the evidence of breakfast on the kitchen counter? That hadn't been there when we'd left on Saturday.

My head started to swim from the effort of putting it all together.

One thing I was certain of by the time I'd finished looking around was that whatever had happened to Nadine, wherever she'd gone, it hadn't been willingly. There were no empty hangers in the bedroom closet, and her luggage set sat undisturbed in a hall closet. On top of that, her makeup bag was lying on the counter beside the sink in the bathroom.

There was no way she'd gone off for days and not taken fresh clothes and makeup. What girl would do that?

The only thing I couldn't find was her purse. That was a big disappointment, because I had it in the back of my mind that if that was in her apartment, it would be strong evidence that she hadn't gone off somewhere of her own free will. Its absence didn't necessarily mean she'd gone somewhere voluntarily, but it weakened the chance that the police would take this seriously if I went to them with my concerns.

I was positive that wherever she'd disappeared to, someone else was responsible. The big question that remained was whether or not she was still alive, and I was trying not to think too much about that.

When I slipped out of the apartment, I pulled the door shut just as I'd found it, so that it looked closed without actually latching. That was partly in case the police did eventually get involved, so they'd find it just the way it had been left, and partly for myself. You never know when a clue will strike you — when you'll realize that some small thing that seemed insignificant at first will take on new meaning or importance. I didn't think there was anything in Nadine's apartment that would need double-checking, but if I changed my mind on that, I wanted to be able to get back in.

I was almost to the front entrance when a door swung open. It was the crazy landlady, and she startled me so badly that I nearly jumped out of my skin.

"Did you have a good time up there?"

"I was looking for Nadine," I stammered, "but she's not home."

"Not home," she echoed with her weird little cackle. "No better than she should be, that one. Well, you know what they say."

"What do they say?" I must have been almost as crazy as she was to ask.

"When the cat's away and all that." Her eyes narrowed with suspicion. "You were up there a long time. A long, long time. And what do you know? Which way the wind blows?"

I didn't know what to say to that. In fact, it was hard to tell if she even remembered what she was talking about. It seemed as though her brain switched topics randomly, so she might have already moved past the subject of how long I'd been upstairs. If not, though, it was likely that she'd heard me walking around up there, even though I'd tried to be quiet. I couldn't very well act as though I'd been waiting for Nadine to answer the door all that time.

"They're all sorry when it's too late," she muttered suddenly. Her grey curls shook back and forth. "Ask Millie. She'll tell you what happens when you say goodbye to good goody girl." Then she stepped back and slammed the door shut.

I shrugged. Whoever Millie was — if she even existed — I sure didn't know her. Anyway, there was certainly more to worry about than a nutty landlady.

It was a relief to step out of the building into the fresh air and sunshine. Glancing at my watch I saw that I'd better hurry if I was going to be on time for work.

Reaching The Steak Place, I caught the familiar citrus scent near the employee door. It reminded me of the partly eaten orange on Nadine's counter.

For some reason, the thought of that orange plagued me for my entire shift. It must have been the last thing on my mind when I went to bed too, because I had a strangely disturbing dream about Ben and Leo feeding me oranges in the kitchen at work.

Only, in my dream, they kept calling me Millie.

CHAPTER TWELVE

Greg wasn't what you'd call impressed when I told him about what I'd discovered in Nadine's apartment, and how I was now certain that something had happened to her.

"Are you *nuts*?" he exploded, anger clouding his face. "What if someone had been in there? Did you stop to think of that? Did you even so much as stop to *think* of your own safety?"

"No one was there," I said, shaken by his reaction. Greg is always so mild-mannered that it really threw me off to see him so upset. "Anyway, by my estimate, Nadine's been missing for days. It would be kind of strange for someone to kidnap her and then go hang out in her apartment, just waiting to be caught. Be a bit risky, don't you think?"

"What I think is risky is my girlfriend putting herself

in a situation where she could get hurt. Or worse. Let's assume you're right, and someone did take Nadine. Suppose this person had to go back to the apartment for some reason. You walk in and discover the kidnapper and what do you think would happen next?"

"Greg, calm down," I begged. "Nothing happened. Maybe it wasn't the safest thing to do, but at least I know now that she didn't just go somewhere on her own."

"You're not planning to go back there, are you?" he asked, his eyes narrowing suspiciously.

"No. At least, I don't think so."

"You don't *think* so." He sounded disgusted. "Is that supposed to reassure me?"

"Well, how about if I need to go back — which I doubt — I'll call you to go with me?"

"Uh-huh? And if you can't reach me and you just feel you have to go right that minute, then what?"

"I'll wait." I knew I didn't sound convincing. In fact, I didn't quite believe it myself.

"Shelby, this is no joke. If someone took Nadine against her will, you're putting yourself in the middle of a very dangerous situation. It's not petty theft or something. It's the kind of crime committed by someone who's desperate and treacherous."

Listening to him talk I was struck by how serious this whole thing really was. Not so much that it could be dangerous to me, but what was happening to Nadine. I kept trying to convince myself that whatever had taken place, she was still alive. At the same time, I knew full well the opposite could easily be true.

"On the other hand, there could still be a perfectly innocent explanation for her disappearance," he said, but his eyes had shifted so that he wasn't looking directly at me anymore. If you want to convince someone that you really don't mean a word you're saying, avoid looking at them.

"That would be great," I answered, "but I don't believe it. There's been some sort of foul play involved here, and all we can hope is that it's not the worst-case scenario."

"Okay, I can see that you're determined to keep looking into this." Greg sighed — one of those sighs that seems like a question. It wasn't hard to figure out what kind of question he had in mind. No doubt he was wondering how he managed to get stuck with a girl-friend who seems determined to follow trouble around.

"So, what do you have so far?" He sighed again. It was the sound of resignation this time, which was good to hear. The sooner he stopped trying to talk me out of looking into Nadine's disappearance, the better.

"What do you mean, what do I *have*?"

"I know you. You probably have lists of suspects and clues tucked away somewhere by now. Fess up!"

"Okay, from what I know, here's what I think happened. Someone or something made Nadine leave her apartment suddenly, sometime after we worked together on Saturday. By the look of the place, I'm guessing Sunday morning. But wherever they took her, she was still alive later in the day, because she phoned work and quit her job on Sunday afternoon. Only, I think whoever took her forced her to make that call, so no one would be looking for her."

"Do you have any suspects in mind?"

"There's her boyfriend, Leo," I said. "He's the most obvious suspect because, as you know, Nadine just broke up with him."

"Is that it?"

"Well, like I said, Leo is the one with the most likely motive — at least that I know about. But there's also a guy who comes into the restaurant and stares at her. And then there's …"

"Whoa, stop! What's this about a guy who comes into the restaurant and stares at Nadine?"

"Just a customer. It's kind of creepy the way he sits and just looks and looks at her, but he's never said or done anything."

"How old would this guy be?"

"I don't know. Late twenties, early thirties probably."

"You don't know anything about him — like his name or anything?"

"No. Just that he's a customer. I've been kind of watching for him through the window in the door that looks out on the dining room. I haven't seen him so far this week, but then he could have been in when I wasn't working. Hey, I have an idea!" I jumped up, excited.

"I don't doubt that." Greg smiled in spite of himself. "The question is, how safe is it?"

"Well, it's safe for *me*, if that's your worry. Suppose this guy comes in again. I could call you and you could come right over and, you know, follow him to see where he lives or something. Just in case we ever need to send the police to his house."

"I see." Greg looked bemused. "Now, I'll need a few more details on this assignment — like *how* I'm supposed to follow him. I mean, specifically, would I follow him on foot, maybe sneaking through hedges and stuff, or will I need to steal a car out of the parking lot?"

"Wise guy." I swatted him lightly on the arm. "I don't know if he comes by vehicle or not. But, wait! If he's in a car, we just need to get the licence plate number. Then you wouldn't even have to follow him!"

"Uh-huh." Greg leaned back, tilting his chair, and folded his arms behind his head. "You know what scares me about all this, Shelby? Knowing that you're just as likely to go off after some potentially dangerous person on your own."

"I thought the lecture was over," I sighed.

"Yeah, you'd like that, I imagine. No one pestering you about silly little things like whether you're putting yourself in a dangerous spot that could get you killed. What a nuisance I am — bothering you about such insignificant things."

"It's good that you don't exaggerate," I muttered.

"Shelby, listen to me, *please*. For once, bring yourself back to earth and pay attention to the facts of what's going on here. If Nadine's disappearance is due to foul play — *if* it actually is, and *if* you're not just chasing shadows — then this is no game. Have you stopped to think about the reasons she might have been kidnapped or whatever?"

"Well, of course I have! I might just be an amateur detective, but I'm not totally incompetent. I know the importance of understanding the motive."

"So? What are the possible motives then?"

"I think we can rule out kidnapping for ransom. Nadine doesn't come from a wealthy family. So the perp obviously isn't after money."

"The perp?"

"Yeah, perp. Short for perpetrator."

"Of course." He seemed on the verge of laughter, but stopped himself. "Sorry. Go on."

"So, having ruled out money, it looks as though the motive is probably personal."

"And you figure the boyfriend is the most likely suspect in that area."

"Yes, but I haven't ruled out the customer, or, as I started to say earlier, her father."

"Her *father*?" Greg looked astonished.

"Yeah. See, Nadine told me that she's hardly seen her father since she was a little kid. Her parents split up when she was five, and her dad sort of disappeared for years. Now he lives in northern Manitoba, and he keeps asking her to come out there to live. Only, she's not interested. What if he decided to *make* her go there?"

"That seems a bit far-fetched," Greg said.

"I didn't say it was likely. I'm just trying to keep an open mind, you know, not rule anything out. For that matter, I could add Ben, the cook from the restaurant, to the list of suspects. He's always flirting, and maybe she rebuffed him and he didn't like it."

"So, he kidnapped her because she wouldn't flirt with him?" Greg raised an eyebrow as he spoke.

"Well, I'm not saying that any of these guys actually did it, or for those motives," I said, blushing at how silly some of my theories sounded when Greg repeated them in that tone of voice. "I just want to be careful that I don't overlook any potential suspects."

"Uh-huh. So, what's the next step?"

"I'm really not sure. I keep thinking something will come to me, but so far nothing stands out as really important. I'm not sure where to look or who to talk to next. It's just too bad that Nadine's landlady is so wacko, or she might be able to help. Unfortunately, she's out of touch with reality. All you ever get out of her are songs or quotes from old Julie Andrews movies. It's amazing she's even coherent enough to collect the rent! I just don't know what to do next, but I have to figure out something, or any chance Nadine might still have could be gone."

Suddenly, Greg leaned forward so that his nose was almost touching mine and he was looking right into my eyes.

"Sorry to change the subject, but this is the way things are," he said, pausing to kiss me ever so gently. "This situation could be nothing at all, or it could be really serious. Either way, it matters to me because … I love you. Okay? I love you, and I don't want anything to happen to you. So, we're going to have to get some kind of deal going here where I can feel comfortable that you're not putting yourself in places where you could get hurt."

Happiness shoved aside everything else for just that moment, and I found my eyes misting over as I threw my arms around Greg and told him that I loved him right back.

I could barely get myself to concentrate on what he was saying after that, though I vaguely heard myself agree to the precautions he was suggesting.

CHAPTER THIRTEEN

I didn't know Leo's last name or where he lived or anything, so I was pretty proud of myself when I thought
of a way to find him. Remembering that he worked out
at the local gym four times a week, I went over and
watched the door from a bench across the street. Nearly
ready to give up for the day after a few hours had passed
with no sign of him, I was really excited that my plan
had worked when I finally spied him going in.

I'd only seen him briefly a couple of times before, but
I spotted him right off. He walks with a pretty noticeable
swagger, and it seems nearly impossible for him to keep
his hands out of his hair, which is a kind of unnatural
blonde colour. He's one of those people who are con-
stantly running their hands up and through their hair, a
trait I've always found kind of annoying and conceited. I
mean, who needs to fix their hair practically every minute?

It hadn't been my intention to actually talk to Leo if he showed up that day. I'm not entirely sure what my plan was, but that wasn't it. It's just that when he came back out of the gym, especially when I'd been sitting there all that time waiting, with little to do aside from think about what questions I'd ask him *if* I ever got a chance to talk to him, well, all of a sudden I could just see the opportunity slipping away.

It wasn't easy explaining that to Greg later on. I tried, but he was just not seeing reason at that particular moment. In fact, he was making way more of the whole thing than was necessary, if you want my opinion.

Anyway, as I was saying, when I saw Leo coming back out of the gym, a kind of panicked feeling came over me. What if he was indeed the one responsible for Nadine's disappearance, and he decided to take off? I might never have another chance to talk to him. And, in any case, what was he going to do to me, right there on the street with any number of witnesses passing by?

"Uh, hi. Leo, isn't it?" I asked, sidling up to him.

He turned with a smile that faded when he saw how young I was. I realized his first reaction had been to assume I was hitting on him. Gross!

"Yeah?" His voice wasn't that friendly.

"I'm Shelby," I said, nervousness building. "I, uh, worked with Nadine at The Steak Place."

"So?"

"Well, I just wondered if, uh, you've seen her lately." I watched his reaction carefully, but if he was carrying around any guilt, he sure kept from showing it. If anything, he seemed a bit annoyed at being bothered.

"Nope." He took a step, as though to walk away, then hesitated. "Why? Was she lookin' for me?"

"Actually, *I'm* looking for *her*. I haven't been able to find her since she quit her job at The Steak Place. I really need to find her."

"Whoa, whoa. Back up there. Did you say she quit her job?"

"Yes. On Sunday." I tried to tell if his surprise was genuine or not but it was pretty hard. He seemed sincere, but he could have been acting. I didn't know him at all, so I had nothing to compare his reaction to.

He looked at me for a moment and then shrugged. "Well, I haven't seen her," was all he said.

"You seemed surprised about her quitting her job," I blurted, hoping to keep the conversation going. "I take it that she hadn't mentioned anything to you about looking for work somewhere else or anything."

"Nope. In fact, I thought she liked the job there real good. Made a lot in tips and stuff. She never said nothin' to me about quitting."

"Well, I wonder, would you maybe know how to get in touch with either of her parents? I'm guessing they'll know where I can find her." Truthfully, I doubted that her parents knew a thing about Nadine's disappearance, but I really wanted to get in touch with them anyway. I knew that if the police were to be called in, it would be best for her mom or dad to do it.

"All I know is her dad's out west somewhere." Leo looked around impatiently as he spoke. I wondered what his reasons were for so clearly wanting to end the conversation. "Her mom is remarried and lives, I think, in Nova Scotia. Halifax or Dartmouth maybe, I'm not sure. I couldn't tell you what her new last name is, though."

"You don't know her dad's first name?"

"Nope. Look, I gotta get going."

"Okay, well, thanks a lot for your help." I smiled brightly at him, so he'd never guess that he was my prime suspect at the moment. "Oh, is there somewhere I could reach you if I have any more questions?"

"If you have any more questions? What are you, the police?" He laughed and walked off without offering an address or phone number.

It struck me right away that I'd probably been pushing it asking for contact information. Still, it was kind of alarming how immediately he'd made a mental connection between perfectly innocent questions and an official police investigation. Would an innocent person do that?

Of course, Greg was pretty upset when I told him I'd gone to see Leo — he said I'd made a few promises that I wasn't sticking to. I guess that's true, but as I said, I was kind of distracted when I said yes to all that stuff Greg wanted me to agree to for the sake of, as he put it, my protection and safety. Sounded like an ad for a home security system to me.

Really, it was hardly fair for him to ask me to make this big deal right after he'd just told me that he loves me. How's a girl supposed to concentrate when she's all aflutter inside?

"A person would need the memory of seventeen elephants to keep track of all your rules," I told him.

"Shelby, first of all, they weren't, as you put it, *rules*. They were just things to make sure you stay safe. Furthermore, there were only *three* things! *Three*. One: That you wouldn't go anywhere near any of the possible suspects alone. Two: That you wouldn't go back into the apartment by yourself. And three: That you'd let me know where you were going to be at any time you were looking into clues. Isn't it enough that one girl has disappeared? Are you *trying* to be the second?"

"You're getting on my nerves," I said, mostly to cover up my embarrassment. I'm not sure how I got so confused, but I'd have sworn there was a bigger list than that!

"I'm getting on your nerves," he repeated, only his voice had dropped to a really low level and I could hardly hear him. He was shaking his head too.

"Well, you're kind of overreacting," I mumbled.

"That's how you see this? It seems perfectly reasonable to you that you went and talked to Nadine's ex-boyfriend, *all alone*? And *I'm* the one who's making a big deal out of *nothing*. Is that what you're telling me?"

"Maybe it wasn't the smartest thing in the world, but nothing happened," I pointed out. "As you can see, I'm perfectly all right."

"Good, that's great. You didn't get yourself hurt or killed. Keep up the good work. Hopefully, you'll be just as lucky the next time."

I sighed. It was bad enough that Greg was ticked off at me, but the worst part was that it was all for nothing. Going to see Leo had been a waste of time since I hadn't learned anything helpful at all. So, here I was, listening to yet another lecture, and I hadn't gotten anywhere for it.

CHAPTER FOURTEEN

I worked until six o'clock in the evening the day after the big lecture from Greg. Was it ever hard to concentrate on my job. Lisa came in and caught me sitting and just staring off into space a couple of times. She frowned at me and told me to get back to work, but her heart didn't seem to be in it, really. At least her tone wasn't as nasty as usual.

"Where's your head today?" Ben asked me once when I hadn't finished a simple task he'd given me.

"I'm worried about Nadine," I told him. "I can't help thinking something has happened to her."

"Nadine is fine," he said. "You want to know what I think? She met some guy and went off with him somewhere. Happens all the time. She'll be back one of these days, and you'll see you were worried for nothing."

"I wish I could believe that she's okay," I sighed, "but I know in my heart she's not."

"How can you be so sure?" He wiped his hands on the square white apron he wore all the time, came over, and leaned an elbow on my work table, looking at me with concern.

"Because I went to her apartment, that's why. And there was nothing missing. No clothes or make-up or toiletries."

"You have a key for her apartment?"

"No, but I went there the other day and when I knocked the door just opened up. It was shut, but not quite tight."

"Her door wasn't closed and locked?" His voice was tinged with alarm, and I could see that he finally believed that something was wrong.

"No, so, I guess this wasn't really right, but I went in and looked around. Just because I was worried, you know?"

He nodded. "And what did you see in there?"

"Well, nothing really. Like I said, none of her stuff was missing."

"Was there any sign of a struggle?" Ben asked.

"No, nothing like that. But don't you think the fact that she didn't take anything with her proves she didn't plan to go anywhere?"

"The apartment where Nadine lives, are there other people living around?"

"Yes. I don't know if all the apartments are rented,

but she mentioned a couple next door, and the landlady lives downstairs, right underneath her."

"So," Ben smiled, relaxed again. "If something had happened to Nadine, one of the neighbours would have seen or heard something, or there'd be some signs of a struggle. But none of this is the case. No, I think everything is all right."

Just then, the kitchen door swung partway open. I turned, expecting to see Lisa on her way in, but no one was there. I tried to shrug it off, but it gave me an uncomfortable feeling, not knowing if someone had been listening.

Anyway, there was no time to worry about that at the moment, because my mind had started to race with excitement. Ben's casual remark had given me an idea!

After talking to Leo, I hadn't really had anything planned. I was keeping an eye out for the weird customer who'd stared at Nadine, but aside from that, I hadn't known what to do next. Now, I did!

I could hardly wait for my shift to end. The minute it did I raced out the door and hurried over to Nadine's apartment building. Ben was right — if Nadine had been kidnapped, chances were good that someone there either saw or heard something. I wouldn't rest until I'd talked to everyone in the building!

Well, I'd skip the nutty landlady, but then I'd already talked to her the other day. She knew I'd been upstairs to Nadine's place. If she'd known anything about Nadine's whereabouts, I figured she'd have told me then.

I started with the couple that lived in the apartment next door to Nadine's. I knocked on their door twice before anyone answered. It was the wife, and I understood right away why she hadn't answered my first knock. The television was blaring in the next room. I could hear someone buying a vowel so I knew they were watching *Wheel of Fortune.*

"If you're selling something, we don't want it," she said, which I thought was an interesting replacement for "hello."

"No, ma'am. I'm not selling anything." I explained quickly that I was a friend of their new neighbour, and that I hadn't been able to get in touch with her for almost a week.

"I was wondering if you might have noticed, or heard, anything unusual, like the sounds of a struggle," I finished up.

"We mind our own business," she said. "But even if there was a scuffle of some sorts, we'd never hear it. Not with Hank being half-deaf and him having the TV turned up full blast all the time. I don't know why he bothers either. Mostly, he just sits there and complains that there's nothing worth watching anyway."

"This would probably have been late at night last Saturday, or early in the morning on Sunday," I said. "Does your husband have the TV on *all* the time?"

"Well, of course not. We'd have been sleeping at those times, though. I hope you find your friend all right, but I'm afraid we can't help you."

I wished I could flip out a business card and pass it over the way detectives do, saying something like, "Well, if you think of anything, give me a call."

Since I had no cards, I scribbled my name and number on the back of an old receipt in my purse and gave it to her. "This is my phone number," I said. "Would you call me if you happen to remember anything?"

She shrugged and stuffed it into her pocket. I could picture it still being there the next time she threw her pants into the washer.

There were eight apartments in the building. Eliminating theirs, Nadine's, and the landlady's, there were five left to check out.

A middle-aged woman with booze on her breath answered the next door I tried. She talked for what seemed an hour, though my watch said it was only ten minutes. I wouldn't have minded if she'd had anything to say about Nadine, but she chiefly blabbed about how dangerous society is to young women these days. I already had Greg for that kind of speech!

A guy in his early twenties answered the second door. He was friendly and told me he'd met Nadine once in the hallway, but he had nothing helpful to offer by way of information.

I moved downstairs. There was no answer at the next two doors, though I had no way of knowing whether the tenants were out or whether they weren't even rented.

I was pretty discouraged by the time I knocked on the last door. When it was opened by a very elderly gentleman, half bent over and feeble looking, I felt like telling him I'd knocked by mistake. That just goes to show that you should never make assumptions.

"Why, I believe I *did* hear something," he nodded, inviting me inside.

Heart pounding in excitement, I followed him in. He introduced himself as Howard Stanley and we shook hands. Then I took a seat in a big old brown leather chair that smelled faintly of pipe tobacco and waited for him to tell me what he knew.

"It was, let me think, it seems to me it was late last Saturday night all right. Yes, that's exactly when it was, because my daughter came to pick me up for church the next morning, and I recall telling her that I thought the girl upstairs seemed to have had an unwelcome visitor, and that I hoped everything was all right. Only she didn't seem too interested, and when everything was quiet the next day, it went completely out of my mind. Until now, that is."

"Old Ernie there," he lifted a boney finger and pointed to a sleek black cat that was curled up on the floor under the coffee table, "had snuck out. Don't ask me why he does that, because usually he's afraid of his own shadow. Believe it or not, he's terrified when a darned pigeon happens to flutter against the window."

He shook his head sadly. "Did you ever hear of a *cat* that was scared of *birds* before?"

I admitted that I hadn't. For his part, Ernie yawned widely and closed his eyes in a kind of squeeze, the way cats do.

"Well, this one is. Fact is, I should have called him Scaredy-Cat instead of Ernie. Anyway, what was I saying? Oh, yes. The girl upstairs. So, Ernie had snuck out and I'd been outside looking for him. I'd just come back into the hall when I heard someone knock on one of the doors upstairs."

I leaned forward, heart beating in anticipation, hardly able to breathe as he went on.

"And I heard a girl's voice. She sounded surprised more than anything, though there could have been a bit of fright there too. She said, 'What are you doing here?' And here's the strange part, what alarmed me some. Standing as I was, out in the hall, and the stairwell being right next to my door, her voice was as clear as a bell. But I couldn't make out a thing that the other person said. I couldn't even tell if it was a man or woman talking to her.

"Seemed like whatever this person said, though, it must have been kind of persuasive, because there it was the middle of the night, and she says 'Well, come in for a moment then,' only she didn't sound one bit happy about it. If anything, I'd say her voice was reluctant. Then I heard her door close and that was it."

My brain was whirling with all sorts of thoughts when I'd thanked Mr. Stanley and headed home. Mostly, there was a whole new bunch of questions going through my head — and no one to put them to!

CHAPTER FIFTEEN

"Guess what I found out at the apartment building!" I said to Greg, unable to keep the excitement out of my voice.

"What apartment building?" His eyes narrowed.

"Nadine's," I said impatiently.

"*Nadine's* apartment building," he echoed. His voice was a mixture of disbelief and anger.

Then my heart kind of sank, because I realized I hadn't let him know where I was going, like I was supposed to. I almost wished I hadn't stopped at Broderick's Gas Bar on my way back home after talking with Mr. Stanley.

"Oops, sorry," I said. "I guess I forgot to call you. It's just that I was so excited after Ben gave me an idea of what to do next. I guess I got a bit ahead of myself and forgot our deal."

A car pulled in for gas then, and he went to service it. That gave me a moment to compose myself. On the other hand, it also gave him time to get even angrier than he was already.

When he returned he stood silently, waiting. His face wasn't what you'd call happy.

"I really *am* sorry," I said softly. I put my hand on his arm. He didn't pull away, which seemed a good sign.

"So, Ben told you to go to Nadine's apartment …" he prompted.

"No, not exactly. I was telling him how worried I am about her, and he said something about everything must be okay because if there'd been any kind of problem the neighbours would have heard the ruckus. I hadn't thought of talking to the neighbours before then, but I realized right off that it was an excellent idea."

"Calling your boyfriend — that's *me*, by the way — would have been a pretty good idea too."

"Yeah, I know." I tried to put more contrition in my expression, but the excitement of what I had to tell him next was growing in me again. "So, anyway, I went there and talked to all the neighbours. Well, the ones who were home, anyway. There was no answer at two of the apartment doors."

"And what did you find out?"

I filled him in on as much of the conversation with Mr. Stanley as I could remember. When I finished, he asked if I'd gone back into Nadine's apartment.

"No," I said truthfully. I thought of how hard it had been to just walk by her place and I was glad I had. The thought that I might have missed something the first time had tempted me something awful, but I'd somehow managed to resist it and walk past the door without going in. At least I'd remembered *that* part of my promise to Greg.

"I *would* like to go there again, though, when you're available to come along," I said.

"Are you also planning to talk to the people in the other two apartments, assuming anyone's living in either of them?" Greg asked.

"Well, it wouldn't hurt to check, just in case. When *you* can come with me, *of course*," I added virtuously. "It would be worth checking out, though. I mean, look at how valuable the information was that I got from Mr. Stanley!"

"You know, it seems you might be right about Nadine running into some kind of trouble," he said. "In light of that, I think you need to take a hard look at what you're going to do next."

"Well, like I said, I'd like to see the apartment one more time and …"

"What I'm actually trying to ask," he interrupted,

"is: do you have any intention of going to the police with any of this?"

"Of course!"

"*When?*"

"Uh, well, I'm not really sure."

"I was thinking that now would be a good time."

"Right *now?*" I gulped. Somehow, the thought of going to the police didn't appeal to me all that much. I'd kind of been hoping to have a bit more information before I went to them. I was worried that they wouldn't take me seriously and that if I didn't present my concerns right the first time, there might not be another chance.

"You can't keep going around investigating a possible kidnapping, or worse, on your own," Greg said sensibly. "You need to report your suspicions to the police right away."

"I think you might have to be a family member to report someone missing," I said.

"No, in fact, you don't." Greg smiled. "Anyone can report a missing person."

"How do you know that for sure?"

"I called the police station a few hours ago, when it wasn't busy here, and asked." He was clearly pleased that he'd been up to something behind *my* back for a change.

"Why'd you decide to go and do that?" I wondered aloud.

"I decided to go and do that," he said with another smile, "just in case you had this very objection, supposing the time ever came that this needed to be brought to their attention."

With some reluctance, I agreed to go on my way home. It occurred to me that I could ask my dad to go with me, but I ended up dismissing the idea. He's not as nosy or protective as my mom, but he'd certainly have questions about *this*, and when he found out what I'd been up to it wouldn't be good.

He wouldn't hide anything like that from my mom either. He'll keep some things between us, but nothing like this. Greg's lectures would look like pats on the back compared to how my folks would react.

I knew I was going to be facing some kind of consequence when it was all over anyway, but in the meantime the less my folks knew, the better. Otherwise, I'd likely be grounded, and then how would I find anything else out?

A uniformed officer wearing a tag that said "Sgt. Newman" came to let me in when I buzzed at the door, which is always locked in the evening. I put a solemn look on my face and hoped I looked older than sixteen.

"I'd like to report a missing person," I said in my most mature and serious voice.

He asked me a few quick questions. At first I thought he was trying to put me off, but then he took a full statement and told me he'd send a couple of officers to check it out.

I was almost home when I remembered about the spilled pop and my fingerprint in it. I considered going back or phoning to mention it, but it seemed so irrelevant that I didn't bother. The police weren't interested in spilled cola.

I felt kind of relieved as I turned up the driveway and headed for my house. Now I wasn't carrying the burden of this whole thing by myself. The police would surely find out what had happened to Nadine, and, hopefully, return her safely home.

My relief, as it turned out, was short-lived indeed.

Chapter Sixteen

I worked again the next morning, though luckily it was a short shift. I'd been awake late the night before, just lying there in my bed thinking, so it was hard to drag myself out of bed when morning came. I'd slept fitfully at best and woke up more tired than when I'd crawled in the night before.

Ben was working, thank goodness! It was quiet in the place at the moment with just the two of us there. Lisa would be arriving shortly, though, and that would be the end of my relaxed time. Once she came in I always found myself tensing up a little, kind of waiting for her to find something to criticize or nag about. Even though I worked in the kitchen with Ben, it felt as though Lisa was the one who was watching me continually.

"You look a bit bleary today," Ben observed, helping me separate eggs — yolks to be cooked into the filling of lemon pies and whites to be beaten into meringue for the topping. The shells were already baked and lined up on the counter.

"I didn't sleep well," I admitted.

"Not still worried about your friend, are you?"

"Yeah, kind of. But now the police are going to check into her disappearance. I'm hoping they'll find her quickly."

"You went to the police?" His eyebrow arched a bit. I could see from the expression on his face that he still thought I was totally overreacting.

"Yes, and they're going to check it out." I said the last with some satisfaction, since it proved that *they* were taking me seriously.

"Well, good. Then you can stop worrying." He cracked the last egg from a carton, separating it with one hand and tossing the shell into the garbage.

I started to answer, but that crazy moaning and banging in the pipes started up then, startling me and making me drop an egg. It smashed on the floor and I found myself flustered and embarrassed. Even though Ben was easy to work with, I still found that his speed and efficiency sometimes made me feel slow and clumsy around him.

"It's just an egg." He smiled, passing me a roll of paper towel.

"I'm glad I'm not working with Carlotta today." I

knelt to wipe up the spreading slime. "She hates it when I make mistakes."

"Oh, no. My dear cousin Carlotta *loves* to see someone make a mistake," Ben laughed. "It gives her a chance to be nasty, which is the thing she likes most in the whole world."

Then he did a hilarious imitation of Carlotta, telling me I was a stupid girl, waving his hands in the air the way she did, and sighing in a deep, heavy way.

"You think it's bad working with Carlotta," he added, "you should try *living* with her!"

"You two live in the same place?" I asked, astonished.

"We three," he corrected. "Believe it or not, I'm crazy enough to share a house with Carlotta *and* Lisa. It's temporary, until we get the family business built up. Am I not the bravest man you ever met?"

I agreed that he certainly was, and he did another imitation of Carlotta, only this one was of her first thing in the morning, grouchy and dishevelled.

We were still laughing when Lisa appeared in the doorway a few moments later. I didn't know if she'd just arrived or if she'd come earlier and been in the dining room. Whatever the case, I sure hoped she hadn't heard Ben's impersonation. Since they were all related she might overlook Ben making fun of Carlotta, but it was different for me. I was an outsider, and already not her favourite person, although I had no idea why she seemed to dislike me.

If she'd heard what Ben had said, she ignored it, turning her attention to me.

"The janitor was sick last night," she said. "I need you to help out here. Come."

I followed her to the dining room and was given brief instructions to vacuum there and then clean the bathrooms. Vacuuming was slow because I had to move all the chairs and then put them back. I could feel Lisa watching me, and I didn't doubt that she was thinking I was taking too long.

I was actually glad to get to the bathrooms, since I was out of her sight in them. It didn't take long to give the toilets a quick scrub with the brush and wash the sinks and counters. I sprayed the mirrors with foaming cleanser and shone them with a clean cloth. Peach air fresheners sat on the counters and I checked to make sure they didn't need to be replaced. Then the floors had to be mopped and I made sure the paper towel and toilet paper supplies were filled.

"I'm finished," I reported back to Lisa, proud of the thorough job I'd done in both bathrooms.

She checked them and then told me to go back to the kitchen. If she was pleased with my work, she sure didn't mention it.

Because of the extra cleaning I'd had to do, the time left for my own tasks was cut down a lot, which meant I really had to hurry. Two o'clock arrived before I knew it and I still had a few things that weren't quite done.

"I'll finish up." Ben waved away my concerns. "You're probably anxious to see what the police found out about your friend."

He was right — I had been thinking about that. I thanked him, folded my apron, and managed to slip out the employee door without any more unpleasant contact with Lisa.

The walk to the police station took about twenty minutes from the restaurant so it was close to two-thirty when I got there. I asked for Sergeant Newman and was told to have a seat. By the time he came to fetch me, it was well past three.

"Sorry about the wait, Miss Belgarden," he said, ushering me into a room with a desk and chairs. I seated myself and waited expectantly. To my surprise, he stopped in the doorway.

"Now, let's see, Officers Monray and Doucet went out on that call," he said. "I think both of them are here at the moment. I'll just fetch whichever one I can find and let him fill you in."

I waited another few minutes and then an officer came sauntering in.

"I'm Officer Doucet," he said, shaking my hand.

110

He gave me a friendly smile and then flipped open a black notebook.

"Have you found out anything about Nadine?" I asked.

"It says here in my report," he said, without answering my question, "that you had gone to Miss Gardiner's apartment before you filed a report with us. Is that correct?"

"Yes."

"Could you tell me again what you found at her apartment?"

I went over it in as much detail as I could think of at the moment, puzzled as to why he was asking me this. The thought of the spilled pop with my fingerprint in it popped into my head and I explained about that too. He didn't seem at all interested in that part, so I figured I was being a bit paranoid.

"Now, it says here that when you left Miss Gardiner's apartment, you didn't secure the door."

"No. I left it the way it had been before," I said. "It looked like it was closed tight, but it wasn't, not quite, and the lock hadn't latched. When I knocked, the door opened on its own."

"Uh-huh. Well, when we went to investigate, we found the door closed and locked. We had to get the landlady to let us in." He smiled briefly, and I wondered what weird performance he'd been subjected to in order to gain access to the apartment. At least he wouldn't have been accused of being Mary Poppins.

"It seems that wherever your friend was," he went on, "she'd gone back to the apartment between the time that you were in there and when we went."

"Nadine was there?" I gasped.

"No, but she'd been there. In fact, I see that you checked whether she'd taken anything with her or not, and she hadn't at that time. That was pretty good thinking on your part." He smiled again. "In any case, when we went, her suitcases were not in the closet where you'd seen them, and a lot of her clothes were missing."

I sat very still, absorbing this news.

"Her makeup and toiletries were gone too." He flipped the book closed again. "So, it looks like your friend is fine. Unfortunately, she isn't being very thoughtful about letting people know where she is, but she's been to the apartment to get some of her things."

"But where *is* she?" I asked aloud, not really meaning to.

"Most of the time, in situations like this, there's a guy involved. Girl meets up with someone, they hit it off, and she up and goes off with him somewhere. She'll probably show up again in a couple of weeks or so, or she'll come for the rest of her things. Either way, you can stop worrying about her."

He asked me if I had any questions. When I said I didn't, he stood, told me I'd done the right thing in reporting my concerns, and said he was glad things had turned out okay. He walked me to the door, where he shook my hand again and told me to come back and ask for him if I had any further concerns.

All the way home I told myself that I should be feeling a lot better.

I wasn't.

CHAPTER SEVENTEEN

"You know what? I bet that the person who was at Nadine's door that night, when she said 'What are you doing here?' was an old boyfriend!" Betts's eyes lit up as she offered her theory. "And the reason the old guy couldn't make out an answer was because ... they were kissing!"

"Possibly," I said, though I know doubt crept into my voice.

Betts and I were facing each other, seated on the big double swing in her backyard, where I'd gone after finding my own house deserted. I'd phoned Greg's place to tell him the news and to see if he had any ideas on the subject, but Dr. Taylor told me he'd been called into work.

"Yeah," she said dreamily. "They could have broken up over some silly fight, like I did with Derek, but they always kept loving each other. And then, finally, he couldn't take it anymore and he came crawling back, just like Derek did."

The "romantic" image she was trying to paint didn't quite fit the way I saw her and Derek — the Squabble Champions! I tried to be fair and consider her idea on its own merits, aside from the unlikely comparison.

"So, how did he find her?" I asked.

"Huh?" Betts shifted back to reality with some difficulty. "What do you mean?"

"Nadine had just moved into a new apartment, remember? She didn't have a phone hooked up or anything yet. How would an old boyfriend have found out where she was living?"

"Uh, he could have asked a mutual friend."

"Possibly," I repeated, no more convinced than I had been earlier. "But then, why didn't she take anything with her when she first went off with him? Why wait a week to come and get her stuff?"

"I don't know. Maybe she didn't know how long she'd be gone the first time. Or maybe she had stuff kicking around his place from when they used to go out before. Or maybe he's rich and he just bought her new things to tide her over for a while."

I was pondering these suggestions when she interrupted my thoughts.

"*Why* are you doing that?"

"Doing what?"

"That thing with your eyebrows."

I realized I was arching my brows, though it had been entirely unconscious. I stopped.

"I know what it means, you know," she went on. "You just assume automatically that I'm wrong. Probably you think you're the only one who can figure things out, just because you got lucky with a couple of other crimes. Well, you know what I think?"

"What?" I asked, startled at the sudden outburst.

"I think you're just inventing things in your head so you can run around playing the big detective."

Betts's accusation was unexpected, and it stung. It echoed something Greg had said a while back, though he'd been teasing. I began to wonder if there was some truth in it. After all, the police were satisfied there was nothing to worry about, and they were trained for that sort of thing.

"Betts, I hope I'm not doing that," I said, trying to keep from getting angry. "I'm just worried about Nadine, that's all. And I want to make sure she's okay."

She shrugged. "Anyway," she said, "like the cop told you, she went and got her stuff, and that had to happen since you were in the apartment, so there's really nothing to worry about."

"I just wish I knew *when* her things were taken from her place, or if *she* was actually the one who got them."

"Why, what's the difference?" Betts was clearly bored with this conversation and ready to move on.

"Well, what if someone else came and took her stuff, to make it look like she was okay?"

"Why wouldn't they just do that in the first place then? Why wait for a week or so?"

I didn't answer, but that was mainly because I was thinking. Maybe there was a way to find out if it had actually been Nadine who'd gone to get her things. It was just yesterday when I'd talked to the tenants who'd been at home, so it wasn't likely that any of them would have anything to add, but there were still the two apartments where I hadn't gotten a response. And there was the crazy landlady. It wouldn't do any harm to talk to her. Who knows, she could be clearheaded for a change.

Of course, there was a bit of a problem since Greg was working at the moment. I knew that Betts and Derek had plans in a little while, so she wouldn't be able to go along either. If I went alone *again* Greg was going to flip out, and I sure didn't want to have to hide it from him. I also didn't want to wait!

An idea popped into my head then. It was a bit devious, but basically harmless. I stood up and steadied the swing so I could step off it.

"I think I'll stop over at Broderick's to see what time Greg gets off work," I said. "I guess you have to get ready for your date with Derek anyway."

"Yeah." She perked up a bit. "Well, I'll see you later. And stop worrying about Nadine, I'm sure she's okay."

"You're probably right," I agreed, trying to sound like I meant it. After all, that would be good practice for what I was about to do.

As soon as I got to Broderick's, Greg's face lit up like it always does when he sees me. I admit I kind of get butterflies in my stomach every time I see him too.

"Ah, fair damsel," he greeted me, with a mock bow followed by a quick hug. "I thought you were at the mercy of your heartless taskmasters today."

"I was, but it was a short shift. What time do *you* get off?"

"Not until closing," he said, "so any sleuthing you have planned in that stubborn head is going to have to wait until tomorrow."

"Actually, that's all over," I said with what I hoped looked like a smile of relief. "I went to see the police after work and they told me that Nadine's fine. She's been to her place to get some of her stuff and everything."

I must have looked convincing because Greg didn't even seem suspicious. He hugged me hard then and said that was *great*, and that I must be really relieved.

"Oh, yes!" I agreed, with my smile frozen on. Already, guilt was nagging at me. It wasn't as though I was actually lying to him though, was it? After all, that *was* what the police had said, and just because I didn't necessarily believe everything was okay, that didn't mean *I* was right.

"So, I guess I can close this case," I added innocently, "though there are a couple of things I want to find out — just to, you know, tie up a few loose ends."

"Yeah? What kind of things?"

"Well, not much. I think I'll stop over and see if the crazy landlady happens to know when she'll be back. Just little things like that."

This time Greg didn't seem the least bit concerned that I was going back to the apartment building alone. Why would he? As far as he was concerned, the whole matter was resolved, Nadine was safe and sound, and I'd been worrying for nothing all along.

I left the gas bar a few moments later, forcing myself to saunter along in the most casual way until I was out of Greg's sight. Then I started speed walking so I'd get to the apartment building as quickly as possible.

CHAPTER EIGHTEEN

Guilt was really starting to do a number on me by the time I reached the apartment building and stepped inside the gloomy hallway. No matter how much I tried to tell myself that I hadn't *actually* lied to Greg, I knew I had.

What I'd told him about the police was true enough — to a point — but the rest of it was an out-and-out lie. I wasn't at the apartment to ask the landlady when Nadine was coming back — I was there to continue looking into her disappearance.

I pushed those thoughts aside for the moment and headed to one of the two apartments where no one had answered on my last trip. This time the door opened almost immediately and I found myself facing a burly giant of a man. He stood around six feet four and had long hair, a full beard, and the most massive hands I've ever seen. His shoulders seemed to span the full width of the doorway and muscles bulged out on his arms, stretching the fabric of his T-shirt sleeves.

"Yeah?" His voice was deep and sounded a lot like an animal growl.

"I, uh …" I tried to speak, but my words seemed to get stuck in my throat.

"You sellin' cookies or sump'n?" he asked. At the same time, he reached behind him, his hand dipping into a pocket and coming out with a worn black wallet.

That act seemed to give me back my courage. I figured if he was the sort who buys cookies and stuff from kids then he probably wasn't as scary as he looked.

"No, I'm not selling anything," I said quickly. I suppose I should have been insulted that he thought I was a little kid out selling Girl Guide cookies, but I was too relieved to think about that just then.

"Actually, I'm looking for a friend of mine. Nadine Gardiner. She lives in this building."

"Well, she don't live here," he said, shoving his wallet back into his pocket. "Must be one of the other apartments. Here, it's just me and Echo, the talking parakeet that don't actually talk, though I paid for a bird that kin talk. Got ripped off, I guess, though I s'pose I could take him back. He came with a guarantee but you know how it is. Dumb things look at you with their heads cocked to one side a few times and you feel like they're attached to you. Truth is, only thing a bird cares about is did you buy the kind of seed they like."

A thought flashed through my head about Mr. Stanley's nervous cat, Ernie, and I almost laughed imagining how frightened he'd be if he knew there was a bird living just down the hall from him! Poor Ernie would probably spend his days hiding under the bed.

"No, no," I hastened to explain, "my friend lives upstairs. But she's been missing, or, at least I haven't been able to find her, for about a week now."

"Missing?" He frowned. "Don't her folks know where she is?"

"She lives alone," I said. Then I went over it all real quick — what had happened. It seemed odd, talking so casually to this enormous guy who, quite frankly, looked kind of dangerous.

"So, she's older'n you?" he asked.

"Yes. We work together, at the new restaurant, The Steak Place."

"I know the place," he nodded. "I go in there for takeout pretty regular since I work nearby a few nights a week and I like to get a feed before the place closes. My own shift doesn't end until a bit later, and I get pretty hungry." He patted his ample girth as if to prove it. "Anyway, I'm off track here. Did you say you called the police?"

"Yes." I nodded and filled him in on what they'd found.

"Hungh," he grunted. "Could be just like they said, or it could be another way altogether."

"That's why I'm asking people in the building if they heard or saw anything."

"Wish I could help you," he said, "but it just happens that I been away now for, oh, must be two weeks I s'pose. Just got back to town day before yesterday, picked up Echo, and came home. So, I wasn't around when your friend went missing."

"And you haven't happened to notice a young woman — or anyone else — carrying a suitcase in the hallway, since you got back?"

"'Fraid not. Sorry."

"Well, thanks very much for your time," I said. I paused, a little hesitant about the idea of offering this guy my phone number, though he'd been nice enough. He solved the quandary for me though.

"Hang on and I'll get you my card," he said, "'case you have any more questions or whatever. If you want, you can leave your number too. I'll be more'n happy to call if I remember anything, or if I see your friend."

It surprised me to hear that he had a business card. It sort of lent him a bit more respectability than his appearance and manner of speaking had. And he *had* seemed genuine in his desire to help, even though he didn't know anything. I decided to go ahead and give him my name and number.

I jotted them down on a sheet in the little coiled memo book I'd started carrying around after the last time I'd been there and had to use an old receipt. Not at all sure if I was doing the right thing, I tore out the page and passed it to him when he returned with a business card. I glanced at the name on it.

"Well, thanks again, Mr. Elliot."

"Anytime," he said, thrusting out his hand, "and call me Neil."

I shook his hand, slipped his card into my pocket, and went on to the next apartment.

I knocked twice and waited for a few minutes before giving up on anyone being home there again today. I was still standing there, wondering if the apartment was even rented, when a voice behind me made me jump so high it's a wonder I didn't bang my head on the ceiling.

"You won't find anyone there, missy."

I whirled around to find myself facing the landlady. She was in fine form, wearing a brightly flowered housecoat and fluffy pink slippers. Her grey hair looked as though it hadn't seen a comb in several days.

I had to swallow hard and take a couple of deep breaths before my heart stopped pounding from the fright she'd given me. How she managed to walk so silently on these creaky old floors was beyond me, but I sure hadn't heard her coming. Maybe she knew exactly where to step, or maybe her frail little body didn't put enough pressure on the boards to make them creak.

"Is this apartment empty then?" I asked when I could speak again.

"Been empty for months," she nodded. "I don't like to see anyone take it either, haunted as it is."

"Haunted?" I echoed.

"Haunted something terrible," she said, her head bobbing up and down again. "You don't want to go in there, believe me."

"What makes you think it's haunted?" I asked.

"Oh, I hear the sounds, the groans and screams," she whispered, leaning forward so that her face was almost touching mine. "They think I don't know they're in there, but I know all right."

"*When* did you hear these screams?" I asked, a chill of fear running through me.

"When, you say? When? I'll tell you when. First thing nearly every morning. They're in there all right, screeching and moaning, only when the police went to look, they couldn't find anything. But they're there all right. They're there."

As I realized that she hadn't heard anything related to Nadine's disappearance, I felt incredibly stupid for having listened to her craziness in the first place. It seemed a bit unlikely that there'd be a single unit in the whole place rented if there was daily screaming and moaning in one of the apartments. Obviously, it was another of her nutty imaginings.

"Well," I said, humouring her, "it's good that there's no tenant in there then."

"Say, you're the same one that was here before," she said. "For the girl upstairs."

"Yes, I am," I said. "In fact, I was wondering if you might have seen her in the last few days."

"I told you," she said, keeping her voice low, "to ask Millie about that."

"Oh, yes, I forgot to talk to Millie," I said brightly. "I'll get right on that, then." As embarrassing as it is to admit this, I'd already asked around to see if anyone knew someone named Millie, just in case there was some clue there. Of course, I'd come up blank.

She nodded, as though we were co-conspirators. Then she slid noiselessly back down the hallway and into her own apartment, closing the door just as silently.

I considered going back around to the other apartments to ask if anyone had seen Nadine taking suitcases out since I'd talked to them yesterday, but it was getting a bit late and Mom and Dad would be worried about me if I didn't soon get home.

I can always check on that tomorrow, I thought. To be perfectly honest, I was starting to doubt myself. I wasn't one hundred percent sure that the door hadn't been closed tight when I'd been there yesterday, so I couldn't be certain whoever took Nadine's things had done it in the last twenty-four hours. When I'd been there yesterday, it had looked the same as I'd left it, but since I hadn't actually gone inside, I couldn't be absolutely sure.

The only thing I was really sure about was that I seemed to be getting nowhere in my search for Nadine.

Chapter Nineteen

A nagging conscience isn't something you can get away from, and mine was bothering me something terrible by the time I got home that night.

It might have been because I hadn't found out anything new on my trip to the apartment building, which meant I'd lied to Greg for absolutely nothing. I could well imagine how he was going to react when I told him the truth, and I wasn't looking forward to it one bit, let me tell you.

Well, there was no sense worrying about it in advance. I checked in with my folks then grabbed a banana, some peach yogourt, and a glass of milk and went up to my room. Once I'd had my snack, I took out my notebook and jotted down what I'd done that evening, though it made a sad-looking entry indeed.

I didn't suppose it would hurt to look over the other notes I'd been keeping since Nadine disappeared, so I flipped through the book and reread everything I had. Some of it seemed to make little sense, and other things looked like potential clues, but they didn't necessarily fit with one another.

It was all very frustrating.

I booted my computer then, thinking to do some kind of research that might be helpful, but when I went online, all I could do was sit there and stare at the search engine. I'd have liked to get some suggestions that might help my investigation, but I had no idea where to start. Besides, my stomach was all tied up in knots.

I checked my email then and found a message from Greg. It was a sweet, funny little note that only served to make me feel even worse. I sent him an answer in case he checked his mail when he got home that night, then went back to staring blankly at the monitor, waiting for inspiration to strike me.

After a few fruitless moments passed, I suddenly thought of the business card that Neil Elliot had given me. Curious as to what kind of work he did, I pulled it out of my pocket and examined it.

The print under his name was small and dark, tiny raised bumps in the centre of the card. It said simply: "Professional Services." That didn't tell me a thing about what he did.

I shrugged, stuck it in my desk drawer, and went back to looking at the monitor. After a few moments I reached over, meaning to shut the system off. That's when an idea came to me, though I have to admit it was one of the lamest ideas I've ever had.

I tapped a few keys, typing in the words "Julie Andrews movies," and then pressed enter. Seconds later the search engine brought back eighty-seven hits. I scrolled through them, selected one that seemed to offer a complete list of all the movies the British actress had ever made, and clicked on it.

I'd seen Julie Andrews in *The Princess Diaries* a few years before and knew she'd starred in *Mary Poppins* and *The Sound of Music*, but I'd never seen them and that was all I'd ever heard of her acting in. I was surprised to see a fairly long list of movie titles. I guess if the nutty landlady spends her days watching movies that Ms. Andrews is in, well, it's nice that she has a variety.

"This is not going to help me find Nadine, that's for sure," I said to myself, feeling ridiculous. Still, I couldn't think of anything else to do. Since the landlady is apparently obsessed with this actress, most of her remarks seem to be related to one of Julie Andrews's movies. To understand any potential clues in what she'd said, I'd need to go to the reference point, namely, whichever movie she was talking about at the time.

As unlikely as it seemed, I decided that if there was *any* chance that something she'd said could even point me toward a clue, it was worth a shot. The first thing I'd have to do would be to find out if any of the movies happened to be about a haunted apartment. That was what she'd been raving about tonight anyway.

The task looked like it would take a while, considering that I'd have to check out the synopsis of each film. Even then, it might need further research before I'd get the details I was looking for, and at that point the most likely scenario was that it would turn out to mean absolutely nothing.

I sighed and scanned down through the list. Maybe there'd be a movie called *The Haunted Apartment* or *Moaning in Apartment D* or something like that, something that would tell me exactly where to look before I spent hours wasting my time.

Well, there was nothing like that, but my eye was suddenly caught by a 1967 title anyway. My heart sped up a tiny bit, even though it wasn't related to what I was looking for at the moment. It was called *Thoroughly Modern Millie*.

Twice, the landlady had referred to someone named Millie. Not trusting my memory, I glanced through my notebook to see exactly what she'd said: *Ask Millie what happens when you say goodbye to good goody girl*. Excited, I clicked on the title. What I found out was, as

I should have expected, a big disappointment. Still, I made a few brief notes about the plot, just to feel like I was doing something: *Set in the 1920s at a women's hotel, the main character, Millie, has a friend who vanishes. Millie's boyfriend disguises himself as a woman and moves in, in order to help her investigate her friend's disappearance. They discover that the woman in charge of the hotel is an opium addict and is selling the girls into white slavery in order to support her habit.*

I made a mental note to make sure no one ever saw my notes on this whole thing. They'd think I'd gone right off the deep end for sure.

It's true that the movie was about a girl disappearing, but there was no way there was anything related in the rest of it. If anything, putting any stock in a crazy woman's strange remarks was a pretty pathetic indicator of how this whole investigation was shaping up.

I did get a smile at the thought of Greg dressing up as a woman, like Millie's boyfriend had, but thoughts of him reminded me again of what I had to confess the next time I saw him.

It was also kind of amusing to realize that if I took the movie plot as an actual clue, the landlady would have just framed herself, since it would mean *she* was behind Nadine's disappearance. She was nutzoid all right, but I was pretty sure she wasn't an opium addict who'd sold Nadine into white slavery.

I sighed, looked half-heartedly through the list again, and then shut down my system.

Maybe, if I still had no real clues, some other day I could check all of the movies carefully to see if there was a mention of a haunted apartment, but at the moment I was too tired and discouraged.

I felt no closer to finding out what had happened to Nadine than I had been when I first discovered she was missing. Worst of all was the knowledge that since the police didn't believe there'd been any foul play, *I* was the only one looking for her.

Wherever she was, I hoped and prayed that she was still alive. And that I'd find her in time.

I showered, dried my hair, and took the remains of my snack to the kitchen. I put my glass into the sink and dropped the banana peel and empty yogourt container into the garbage can.

As I did, something seemed to click in my head, but before an idea could fully form, it slipped away again.

CHAPTER TWENTY

I was pretty distracted at the restaurant the next day, which was especially unfortunate since I was working with Carlotta.

"What you thinking?" she demanded once, when I'd absentmindedly put a tray of glasses through the dishwasher a second time by mistake. "Maybe you like to pay for hot water from paycheque?"

"Sorry," I mumbled, for once thankful for the racket in the pipes. The unearthly groans weren't enough to drown out her voice though, and she spent a good ten minutes berating me for my apparent laziness, stupidity, and general uselessness. I tuned her out.

It was just a little past three when he came in. I'd gone out front to get a piece of pie for Carlotta, happy at the thought that at least she couldn't growl at me when she was eating. I was just about to push through the swinging door that led back into the kitchen when I saw him out of the corner of my eye.

For a second I froze, as the guy who'd made Nadine so nervous with his incessant staring walked in and sat down at a table. Ruth was the waitress on duty, and she began to cross the room to take his order.

I realized that I was gawking at him and quickly averted my eyes, trying to think of some reason not to leave the room just yet.

I deliberately knocked the fork that I'd sat on the edge of the plate onto the floor. After I'd squatted down and picked it back up, I returned to the station where supplies of clean glasses and cutlery were stored. I dropped the fork into the soiled cutlery section and took a fresh one.

Having stalled as long as I could, and aware that Lisa was watching me with her usual frown, I made my way back to the kitchen, pushing slowly through the door.

"You get lost looking for pie?" Carlotta asked, snatching the plate from me. "Or maybe you just like waste time."

"You're welcome," I muttered under my breath. With one of the suspects in the next room, I wasn't in the mood for her grouchy comments.

"What you say?" she asked. "Maybe you like to say again so I hear. Or maybe you only *brave* when I no hear you."

"I said *you're welcome*," I repeated, this time plenty loud.

She looked both startled and confused at that, and I might have been amused by her expression except my mind was racing trying to figure out what to do about the guy in the next room.

"You no be smart to me," she huffed after a moment, but she seemed deflated somehow, and without following her remark with the usual harangue, she turned her attention back to the pie.

Gathering up my courage, I walked back out into the dining room and approached Lisa, who was standing at the cash register. That was also where the phone was, which didn't help things.

"May I use the phone, please?" I asked, wondering how I was going to ask her to leave the area so I could speak privately.

"You want to make a personal call on work time?" she asked coldly.

"Yes, ma'am, I do. I wouldn't ask, but it's really important."

"If you're more than a few minutes, it will count as your break," she said.

"Yes, thank you," I said. I looked at her pointedly.

She seemed to understand my unspoken message because she moved away from the cash, but after taking a couple of steps, she turned and asked me to pass her the key from the cash register.

What does she think, I'm going to stand here and rob the cash in front of her? I wondered, but I reached over and turned the small silver key that was protruding from the register, pulled it out, and dropped it into the palm of her outstretched hand.

I dialled Greg's number, praying he'd be there. His dad answered on the second ring.

"Dr. Taylor, this is Shelby," I said quietly. "Is Greg home?"

"He sure is. I'll get him for you."

"Thank you." I breathed a sigh of relief. Then I waited what seemed like ten minutes but was probably only one or two.

"Hello?"

"Greg," I said, dropping my voice as low as possible, "it's me."

"Hi, you," he whispered back.

"Listen, I need your help. And I don't have time to explain."

"Okay," he said.

"I'm at work and that guy is here, the one I told you about before."

"The one who stares at Nadine?"

"Yes, him. Remember what we talked about you doing?"

"What, you mean your idea about me following him?"

"Yes. Can you do it?"

"Are you serious? I thought this whole thing was settled."

"I kind of lied to you, sort of. But can we talk about that later? I *really* need you to do this for me."

I heard a heavy sigh, which was impossible to read. It might have been exasperation or anger or disappointment. I was pretty sure it wasn't admiration.

"*Please*, Greg," I implored.

"What's he wearing?"

"Jeans and a light grey polo style shirt."

"I'll see what I can do, but I'm not promising anything."

"Thank you, Greg," I said. "Will I see you this evening?"

"Well, it sure sounds like we need to get together and talk about a few things," he said with another sigh. "Call me when you get home."

"I will," I said. "Bye then." My throat was constricting and I felt like I was about to cry. He'd sounded so totally fed up, his tone of voice colder and more remote than I'd ever heard it before. And yet, in spite of that, he'd still been willing to help me when I asked.

I felt absolutely horrible about the whole thing. The thought of facing him made a cold lump start to form in the pit of my stomach.

I sat the phone back into the cradle and turned to go back to the kitchen, tears threatening to fill my eyes. From beside the waitress station, Lisa stood watching me.

"You can take the rest of your break now," she said softly as I began to pass her with my head down so she couldn't see that my eyes were brimming.

The unexpected kindness was enough to put me over the edge. I managed to squeeze a quick thank you out and then hurried to the staff room in the back, where I burst into tears.

When I emerged ten minutes later, the guy had finished his pie and gone. I had no way of knowing whether or not Greg had gotten there in time to follow him.

To Carlotta's great joy I worked like a madwoman, determined to keep busy for the rest of the shift. The faster the time went by until I could find out what had happened, the better!

CHAPTER TWENTY-ONE

I'd been expecting Dad to pick me up after work so it took me a few seconds to realize that Greg was sitting in the parking lot in his father's car. I hurried over, hoping I didn't smell too much like onions, which I'd been chopping just a few moments before I finished my shift.

"My dad is supposed to be picking me up today," I said, leaning down to the driver's window.

"I know. I was talking to him a while ago and I told him I could get you instead."

"You were talking to my dad?" I gulped. "You didn't tell him anything about, you know, Nadine and stuff, did you?"

"You mean did I rat you out to your folks?" He shook his head in disbelief. "No, Shelby, I didn't."

"I didn't really think so," I said, though I was

actually relieved. "So, how'd it happen that you were talking to my father?"

"I saw him coming out of Stoneworks right after I finished following that guy for you."

"So you *did* get here in time!" I said. "Well? What happened?"

"Are you going to get in," he asked, "or will we just have this whole conversation with you leaning in the window?"

I went around to the passenger side and slipped into the car. Facing Greg, I smiled in what I figured was a pretty darned alluring way, thinking a kiss would go a long way toward smoothing things out between us, but he didn't take the hint.

"Okay," he took a deep breath, "I'd barely gotten here when the guy came out. He was on foot, so I had to park and follow him that way. It's harder than you'd think, even though he wasn't suspicious so he wasn't really looking back over his shoulder or anything. I hung back as far as I could without losing him."

I considered saying something admiring about his cleverness but thought better of it. He *is* smart, which only means he'd see through that kind of flattery in a second.

"So, anyway, I got his address. At least, I assume he lives there, since he went right into the house without knocking."

"Greg, that's *great*!" I said, delighted. "What is it?"

"What is what?"

"The address?"

"Ha! You can't really think I'm just going to pass it over to you."

"What? Why not?"

"Let's see, can we think of any reason that I might not give Shelby the Out-of-Control Detective the address of a possible kidnapper?"

"C'mon," I said, but I giggled anyway, mostly because relief was flooding through me like crazy. It almost made me feel weak. If Greg could still joke with me, then he wasn't as ticked off as I'd feared.

"No, wait! I just thought of a reason. Shelby the Out-of-Control Detective is … how should I put this … out of control!"

"Greg! I'm not that bad."

"You're *not that bad*." The way he said it didn't exactly sound like he was agreeing, I noticed.

"I'm not," I said again. "Anyway, what do you think I'm going to do with it?"

"Who could even *begin* to predict what you might do?" he sighed. "I figure that the safest thing is for me to hang onto this bit of information until it's needed."

"I wonder if he lives alone," I thought aloud.

"See what I mean!" Greg threw up the hand he wasn't using to steer. "You'd go there and snoop around if you knew where he lived. I know you would."

I started to deny it, but the truth was I probably would have done just that. I tried another charming smile instead.

"Maybe we could go there together, later on tonight," I suggested, "and if anyone catches one of us, the other one could, you know, create a diversion or something."

"I wonder if there's any hope for you at all," he mused. He laughed then and reached over and touched my face with his hand, all gentle like.

"I thought you were really mad at me," I said, taking hold of his hand and holding it tight. "I worried all day that we were going to have a big fight or something."

"It's a bit difficult staying angry with you," he smiled. "Don't take that to mean that you can just get away with anything, though. And by the way, I want the whole story of what you were up to last night, and don't leave anything out."

I told the whole story and didn't leave anything out. By the time I'd finished we were at my place and had been sitting in the driveway for about ten minutes.

"So, are you going to forgive me before we go in?" I asked. I leaned toward him and tried to make my lips, you know, kind of full and luscious, though it probably just looked as if I was pouting.

"I forgave you before you started talking," he said. Then he put his arm around my shoulder and pulled me over a bit and kissed me, so I figured I'd managed the luscious look after all.

We went into the house then and Mom and Dad put on this big act to embarrass me, only it didn't work because I was so happy.

"Shelby? Is that you dear?" Mom started. She squinted as though she was straining to see me. "Randall, can you tell if it's her?"

"Why, I think it is, Darlene," he said. "I'm not a hundred percent sure, though. It's so long since I've seen her."

"You saw me *yesterday*," I pointed out.

"What? The back of your head in the hallway doesn't count."

"You've been on the fly ever since school let out for the summer," Mom complained. "Why, we never see you *at all*."

"I was going through the photo albums earlier; made me kind of nostalgic," Dad agreed.

"You two are weird," I observed. "Anyway, what's for dinner?"

"Well, actually, we've already eaten," Mom said. "We have plans with Joy and Terry this evening. But there's honey garlic chicken and a vegetable rice dish in the oven, so you two just go ahead whenever you want."

"Okay, thanks, Mom," I said.

After they'd gone I got the food out of the oven and took it into the dining room to put it on the table. To my surprise, the table was already set with our good dishes and there was a pair of candles as well as a vase of flowers in the centre.

"Hey, this is cool," Greg said coming in behind me. He lit the candles with the matches Mom had left out and we turned out the light and sat down to eat.

It was pretty romantic, really. For a while, I even stopped thinking of ways I could persuade Greg to check out the house where the guy he'd followed lived.

But only for a while.

CHAPTER TWENTY-TWO

"I must be crazy."

"Shhhhhhhhh!" I hissed, though there was no particular reason to be quiet. We were sitting in the car, parked along the street just beyond an evergreen hedge. It bordered the yard around a little white bungalow, which was the house Greg had followed the guy to from The Steak Place.

"Tell me again just exactly what it is that we're looking for?" Greg said.

"Signs that there's something fishy going on in here," I answered impatiently. "Or, if the guy comes out, we can see where he goes."

"Don't you think we're going to attract attention if we sit here for any length of time?"

I hadn't thought of that, but he was absolutely right.

"Besides, suppose Nadine actually *is* being held in

there," Greg said. "It's not as if someone's going to let her come to the front door and wave."

"Maybe one of us should go ask to use the phone or something," I said.

"Good idea. How about you, since this guy has only seen you at work who knows how many times?"

"I've only been in the same room with him twice, and he never paid the least bit of attention to me either time," I said, certain he'd never recognize me. "But anyway, if that's your worry, *you* could go."

"Shelby, this isn't the best thoughtout plan you've ever come up with. Think about it. If I went to the door and asked to use the phone, one of two things would happen. They'd tell me to get lost, which could mean they have something to hide *or* that they don't want total strangers waltzing though their house. Or, they'd let me make a call. And that wouldn't prove a thing either."

"Shhhhh!" I said for the second time. "Someone's coming!"

Sure enough, the side door was opening. My heart quickened when I saw that it was our suspect.

"There he is!" I gasped.

"Yeah, there he is." Greg sounded disappointed.

"Try to keep your excitement under control," I said.

"Well, hon, what exactly do you think we're going to do now? Get out of the car and walk down the street after him? *That* wouldn't look suspicious. Or drive beside him?"

"I'm thinking," I said. "Give me a sec."

"It only takes you a second to come up with a plan?" He smirked. "That explains a lot."

"Oh, I know!" I said, punching him on the arm for his last comment. "We'll drive ahead of him, and you can let me out somewhere that he can't see me. Then I'll walk real slow until he passes me. He'll never suspect I'm following him if I'm ahead of him to start out."

"That's not bad," Greg admitted, "but what will I be doing in the meantime?"

"You can drive around here and cross streets, like you're trying to find a specific place or something. He'd have no reason to think we're connected."

"Okay," Greg agreed slowly, "but don't get too close to him, and if he goes into a building somewhere, you *don't go in*. Walk past it *no matter what*. Promise?"

I agreed and he started the motor. We found a perfect place for him to let me out, a big, old, closed-up Victorian-style house with a circular driveway that went around behind. I slipped out of the car at the back of the house and hurried out to the street. The suspect was still a ways back.

I sauntered along, wondering if Greg had come back out or if he was waiting for the guy to pass the house. He hadn't driven by yet, but I didn't suppose it mattered as long as he was somewhere nearby and would be checking on me regularly.

I sensed rather than heard the suspect approaching, moving up behind on my left. He passed on the outside, closest to the road, and barely glanced at me as he went by.

But then, he paused. I saw the shift in the smooth movement of his steps, so I had a feeling of what was coming before it happened.

He didn't quite stop just then, but he did slow down enough that I'd have had to stop completely to avoid him. Then he turned and looked directly at me.

My knees nearly gave out, which made the next couple of steps I took look a lot like drunken lurches. It was all I could do not to turn and run off screaming for Greg. How I managed to keep myself from it I have no idea.

"Hello, miss," he said. By then he had stopped and he stood facing me.

Where was Greg?

"Hi," I said, hoping I sounded natural and not scared to death, which I was. I could picture him grabbing me, hauling me off into a hedge, and slitting my throat.

"Don't be alarmed," he said reassuringly as he took a step closer.

Alarmed? I just felt like I might wet my pants, is all. I tried to look around for Greg without making it obvious what I was doing. On the other hand, maybe I should make it obvious. If he knew I wasn't alone and entirely at his mercy, he might not be so quick to carry out whatever fiendish plan was forming in his demented head.

"Don't you work at The Steak Place?"

"Huh?" I'd been *so sure* he'd never noticed me there. Wrong.

"I was just asking … I thought you worked at the new restaurant downtown."

"Oh, yeah. I do."

"I thought I recognized you." He smiled, held his hand out, and said, "I'm Paul Edwards. I didn't mean to startle you."

Numbly, I shook his hand and mumbled my name.

"I just," he looked embarrassed suddenly, "I was wondering if you might be able to tell me …" He cleared his throat and avoided my eyes. "That is, I was just curious, one of the waitresses there, the younger woman … well, I haven't seen her the last few times I've been in, and I was wondering if she might be sick or anything."

"Are you a friend of hers?" I asked, summoning my wits the best I could.

"No, no. Goodness, I'm a good deal older than she is. I was just, that is, I was … er, the thing is, she reminds me of someone, so I happened to notice her. And I was just hoping she's not ill or anything like that."

"She reminds you of someone?" I felt suddenly bold and brave and ready to ask him anything that came to mind. "Do you mind me asking who?"

"My sister." A troubled look passed over his eyes. "At least, my sister when she was that age. That's some years ago."

"How old is your sister now?" I asked.

"Well, she's not … you see … that is, she's no longer with us."

"She died?"

"Yes. An accident back when we lived in the city. She was probably close to the same age as the girl in the restaurant at the time. The resemblance is quite striking."

"*That's* why you stare at her!" I blurted.

"That's why I … oh, my … I hadn't realized it was that obvious … oh, my goodness, I feel just terrible. She must think … why, I can't imagine what she thinks." His face had turned crimson.

"Shelby!"

The sound of my name startled me so much I nearly jumped out of my skin. Well, not really, I guess. It felt like I might, though. I whirled to see that Greg had pulled up beside the sidewalk and was leaning across looking out the passenger window.

"Oh, hi, Greg." I managed a weak smile, which I hoped would tell him everything was okay.

"Want a lift to your place?" he asked.

"Yeah, sure. Just a sec." I turned back to face Mr. Edwards.

"I'll explain when I see her again," I promised. "But the truth is; she's kind of disappeared, so I don't know when that will be."

"*Disappeared?*"

The shock on his face sure looked genuine. In fact, everything he'd said had the ring of truth to it. Not just what he'd said, either, but the way he'd said it.

I filled him in briefly, trying to downplay my worries and reassure him that the police thought she was fine. Still, I could tell he was disturbed by the news. He told me that he'd pray for her, and he sounded totally sincere.

"Well," I said to Greg after I'd told him all about the conversation I'd just had, "that was kind of scary, but way worth it. At least I can clear one suspect off my list."

"So, who does that leave?"

"I think maybe I'd better focus on her ex-boyfriend, Leo."

"What's your next move then?"

"That's the problem," I sighed. "I have no idea."

CHAPTER TWENTY-THREE

Greg and I were sitting at the dining room table, talking over our strategy for how to find out where Leo lives, when it hit me. We'd gone through my notebook again, though it seemed like a total waste of time, and all of a sudden, a connection I'd missed popped into my head.

I jumped up as the significance became clear.

"Forget Leo," I said, "because it wasn't him."

"Huh?" Greg blinked in confusion.

I couldn't blame him one bit, since I'd just been going on and on about how essential it was that we focus on Leo — because everyone knows it's usually the spouse. I know that Leo and Nadine weren't married, but a boyfriend is the next closest thing to a spouse, so it put him in the same category.

"It's not Leo," I repeated, snatching up the notebook again. I flipped back a couple of pages and stuck my finger on an item that I'd written there on the night I'd been in Nadine's apartment.

"This proves he's innocent."

Greg read the note then gave me a questioning look that sort of suggested he was wondering if I'd lost my mind altogether.

"See, I checked out the spot on Nadine's floor. It was pop. And it was sticky."

"Yeah?"

"So, I just remembered, she told me Leo *never* drinks pop. He even used to growl at her when she did, so there's no way it's his."

"So? It's probably hers."

"Nope. That's what I missed. Whoever was in her apartment — whoever took her — almost certainly has to be the person who spilled that pop."

"But you just said she drank pop sometimes."

"Yes, but only diet pop. She told me that specifically."

"So?"

"It just occurred to me that it's the *sugar* in pop that makes it sticky. The pop that was spilled on her floor was really sticky, so it couldn't have been hers. Diet cola has no sugar in it."

"Well then, if you're right about this, we're back to where we started," Greg said. "You've eliminated the two best suspects you had."

"Yeah, I know." I was looking at the notebook again, wondering what else had slid right by. Maybe there were other things that carried meaning I just hadn't seen.

"It might be time, Shelby," Greg went on, "for you to consider the idea that there really *hasn't* been a crime committed. It seems, with the two most likely people cleared, that you might want to take another look at the whole thing. My guess is that the police are probably right. Nadine went off, either alone or with a friend, willingly. I bet she's somewhere having a great time while you're torturing yourself worrying about her."

"I don't know," I said slowly. "It's not like I *want* to think that anything bad has happened to her, you know. I just can't seem to shake the conviction that there's something dreadfully wrong."

He sighed and lapsed into silence as I continued rereading through the notebook. The one thing that seemed to nag at me at the moment was the so-called haunted apartment that the landlady had talked about. How that tied in was beyond me, but I decided I was going to trust my instincts.

"I need to go back to the apartment building," I told Greg. "I'm not sure why, but this whole business of a ghost in apartment D is bothering me."

"Okay," he said, picking up the car keys. For some reason I'd been expecting an objection, so it threw me off a bit that he agreed so readily.

As we drove toward the building I found myself picturing what might have happened in Nadine's living room — some kind of struggle that ended with the spilled pop. I vaguely wondered if it was possible she'd managed to spill it on purpose, to leave a clue behind, hoping someone would understand what it meant.

I decided I was letting my imagination go a trifle overboard.

"Shelby?"

"Yeah?"

"Just out of curiosity, do you think the landlady will actually be able to clarify anything for you about that apartment? From what you've told me, she hasn't been all that coherent."

"Oh, no, I'm not planning to talk to her," I said. "I want to ask some of the other tenants if they've heard anything."

The two apartments that were connected to D were Neil Elliot's, right next to it on the ground floor, and the lady upstairs who'd smelled of alcohol. Her apartment was right over top of it.

I decided to start with Neil Elliot, since he'd been pretty co-operative when I'd talked to him before. In fact, I wasn't all that keen to talk to the woman upstairs or listen to her gloom and doom lectures if I could avoid it.

Mr. Elliot answered his door on the second knock.

"Hello there," he said. "How are you making out looking for your friend?"

"Not so good," I admitted, making quick introductions between him and Greg. "I hate to bother you again, and this is going to sound pretty strange, but do you ever hear weird groaning noises in the apartment next to you?"

"Sure, all the time. In fact, I make 'em."

"You make them?" I repeated, astonished.

"Well, not intentionally," he laughed. "When I shower for work in the morning, the pipes start making a big racket. Sounds like someone's bein' killed next door. It only lasts a minute or so, though."

"Noise from the water pipes!" I said. "I can't *believe* I didn't think of that. That happens all the time at the restaurant."

"Hullo? Hullo?" a voice screeched from inside Mr. Elliot's apartment. "Hullo?"

He grinned. "I'm not sure if you were good luck or bad, but just a little while after you left the other day, old Echo here finally said his first word."

"That's great," I smiled back.

"Yup, I sure was proud of him. I gotta tell you though, after half an hour of steady 'hullo, hullo, hullo,' a person could use a bit of quiet."

"Hullo? Hullo?" Echo called.

"It's nice to be greeted at the end of the day, old buddy, but I think we could give it a rest now," Mr.

Elliot called over his shoulder. "This steady squawking is enough to make a fellow jump in his pick-up and head for the hills."

In spite of his words, he was still grinning. I don't think he really minded Echo's repetition.

"Well, I really appreciate your help," I said. "And I'm sorry to have bothered you again."

"No bother at all. I sure hope your friend turns up okay."

"Thanks." I turned to Greg again as the door closed. "I wonder if we could get the landlady to let us into that empty apartment."

Chapter Twenty-Four

"Why do you want to go into an empty apartment?" Greg asked.

"I don't really know. It's probably stupid, but I'd feel better if I could just have a quick look around in there."

"Okay," he shrugged.

"I know it seems like a waste of time. It probably is. But this is where Nadine was last seen, and I'd like to make sure I haven't overlooked anything. What if she was being held captive in this very building? I'm sure other people know about the landlady thinking that apartment is haunted. In that case, they'd know it's never rented, which makes it a ready-made hiding place. That would also explain why no one reported anything unusual to the police, like a girl being dragged to a car or something."

"Anything's possible," he said. He sounded like he thought it was the least possible scenario I'd ever come up with.

"It doesn't look as though she was taken for personal reasons," I said, "and that makes it a lot harder."

"That's true," he said. "If it was a random snatching ... but wait! Nadine knew the person who was here the last night anyone saw her. Remember? The old guy you talked to heard her answer her door and ask, 'What are you doing here?'"

"Oh, that's right." I'd forgotten about that for a moment. The hard thing about figuring out something like this is keeping all the details straight in your head. Being able to recognize what's important and what the clues mean is even harder.

I knocked on the landlady's door. For a second I toyed with the thought of coming up with a story that would make it more likely she'd let us into the apartment. Something along the lines of "I dropped my contact lens and it rolled under the door." In the end, I discarded the idea.

"You again," she said, her eyes narrowing when she saw me standing there.

"Hello," I said in what I hoped was a bright, perky voice. "How are you today?"

Instead of answering, she peered behind me. I realized she was looking at Greg, and I made a quick introduction. He offered her his hand, but she stared at it as it if were covered in slime, and didn't shake it.

"We were wondering," I said, knowing I was wasting my time asking, "about seeing the empty apartment."

"Told you, it's haunted. I don't rent it," she snapped.

"Yes, ma'am, I remember. We didn't actually want to rent it. We were just curious about the noises in there. We wouldn't touch anything. We thought maybe we could find something. You mentioned that the police couldn't seem to find anything to back up your suspicions."

Her eyes narrowed as she thought about this. To my surprise, she shrugged and told us to wait. Greg and I looked at each other but were afraid to speak while she was back inside her place. A moment later she returned with a single silver key on a thin wire ring.

"Don't say I didn't warn you," she mumbled, passing it over.

We thanked her, took the key, and promised to be right back. She looked doubtful.

I don't know what I was expecting inside the apartment, but there wasn't a thing there. Empty rooms with a slightly stale smell — that's all we found. I have to admit I felt kind of foolish standing there.

"Well, so much for that," I said.

"I guess so." Greg kind of patted my arm like you might do with a small child in need of comfort. "At least you know — and you won't be driven crazy wondering if there's anything in here that might have been helpful."

"Yeah, I suppose eliminating things is part of figuring out what happened in cases like this," I agreed. I tried to sound positive about it, but the truth was I felt anything but.

The more I nosed around, the more the whole thing seemed hopeless. I had no suspects, no known motive, and no clues that appeared to be telling me anything. In short, I had nothing except my own belief that something horrible had happened to Nadine. Even the police thought everything was okay.

"Maybe you're right. Maybe it *is* time I stopped chasing after shadows," I said heavily. "I've become some kind of crime junkie, inventing felonies to feed my need for excitement. I'm sneaking around spying on people and bothering strangers for something that only exists in my head."

"Don't be so hard on yourself," he said. But I noticed that he didn't try to persuade me that maybe there was something to the whole thing and he didn't suggest we keep on checking things out.

"Someone who Nadine *knows* comes to her door, surprising her," I said, reviewing the facts aloud. "She quits her job the next day and takes off somewhere. A few days later she stops by her place and gets her things. There's no evidence of a scuffle, nothing broken in there or anything like that. No wonder the police were satisfied that there hadn't been a crime. There *hadn't*! I was the only one who was determined to make something of nothing."

Again, Greg failed to argue with me. That told me more than anything he might have said. He just put his arm around my shoulder and we walked in silence back to the landlady's apartment.

"Thanks very much," I said, passing her back the key. "The apartment is okay. If you check with Millie I think she'll tell you that what you're hearing is just water noises in the pipes."

She seemed to be absorbing this when we left. I slid into the passenger seat of the car and leaned my head back on the rest.

"Is it all over now, really?" Greg asked as he pulled out onto the street. "Are you honestly going to let this go?"

"Yeah, I guess I have to," I said. I wondered how long he'd secretly been thinking I was just imagining the whole thing.

CHAPTER TWENTY-FIVE

The realization that Greg had been humouring me for who knows how long was a huge disappointment to me, and by the time we got back to my place I was in no mood for his company.

"Thanks for taking me all those places," I said the second the car had come to a full stop. I tried to smile naturally, but my face felt strange and twisted. "See you later."

"Well, I'll walk you ..." he began, but I was already out of the car and halfway to our back door.

I gave a quick wave and hurried inside before the hurt look on his face could start to bother me.

By the time I'd had a long soak in the tub, I was feeling a bit better. Maybe I'd been reading too much, or too little, into how he'd acted earlier. No doubt I'd overreacted because I was so frustrated over this whole thing.

"Well, that's behind me now," I said, pulling my bathrobe closed and tying it. I went into the kitchen and made toast and poured a glass of milk, which I put on a tray to take to my room. As an afterthought, I went back to the fridge, looked for a peach yogourt, couldn't find one, and grabbed blueberry instead to add to my snack.

Mom and Dad were in the living room watching TV. I stuck my head in the doorway.

"I'm going to bed now," I said.

Dad turned to me, smiling, but with his index finger over his lips. He nodded toward my mom, whose head was kind of tilted down. She's always falling asleep when they watch stuff on TV. If you try to wake her up and suggest she go to bed, she'll insist that she's watching something. Without fail, she stubbornly says she was just resting her eyes, even if you point out that she was *snoring* only seconds before.

"Shhh," Dad said, then whispered, "your mom is watching TV."

I muffled a giggle as I headed off toward my room. When I reached the doorway, I started to transfer the tray entirely to one hand in order to free the other to open the door. Instead, as I leaned forward, the door slipped open, almost throwing me off balance and making me spill my milk.

It reminded me of how Nadine's door had looked closed tight, but hadn't been, and how that's what had started this whole mess. And now I was kind of fighting with Greg over it, and all for nothing.

I wished I hadn't been so short with him when he'd dropped me off. I'm sure he knew I was upset about something, but I wasn't at all certain that he knew *why*. Guys don't usually seem to be too clued in to what girls think or feel, as far as I can tell.

I remember one time Greg thought I was really mad about something when I was actually sad. It was weird how he was so far off on what I was feeling, when his emotions are pretty obvious to me most of the time. I forget what it was over, whether we'd had an argument or misunderstanding of some sort.

We don't often fight, so it's funny that I can't recall the particulars. All that's really clear in my head is that I was upset, and he totally misread my feelings. Betts tells me it's the same with Derek — that he has no idea what she's feeling when they fight, either.

"If I'm really furious, that's pretty obvious, even to him," she confided once, "but if I'm hurt or sad about something he's said or done, he always assumes I'm ticked off. Can you *believe* guys are that dense?"

I'd believed it all right, but for some reason, I hadn't thought it really applied to Greg. Not that I think he's perfect or anything, but he's sure a lot closer than Derek. I know one thing — Greg would never leave me terrified on a rope bridge and just take off to the other side.

For some reason, the memory of our recent excursion brought back thoughts of Nadine again. That was probably because the thought of Betts's terror that day reminded me of my theory that Nadine had been abducted. If that had been true — that is, if I hadn't imagined the whole silly thing — I can't even begin to think of how scared she would have been, struggling to get away from her captor, wondering where she was being taken and what would be done with her once she got there.

I pushed those thoughts away with some effort, reminding myself once more that none of it was real, that I'd dreamt up the whole thing.

I turned on my computer and checked my email while I ate my toast, hoping there might be something from Greg. There wasn't. All that was in my inbox was a bunch of junk messages, which I deleted without reading.

Taking my yogourt with me, I crawled into bed and opened the book I was reading. It was actually one Greg had lent me, called *Shoulder the Sky,* and I'd taken it a bit reluctantly because it seemed like a guy story. Turned out that it was really awesome, though, and I'd gotten totally into it.

Tonight, however, it was almost impossible to concentrate on what I was reading, in spite of how good the story was. I kept thinking about Greg and the hurt look on his face when I'd practically jumped out of the car — without kissing him goodnight or inviting him in for a few minutes.

So what if he hadn't been convinced that Nadine had really been kidnapped? He'd still been nice enough to help out, and he hadn't made fun of me over it or anything like that.

I really wanted to call him, but it was too late to phone his house by then. Besides, my folks have never given in and let me have a phone in my room, so I'd have had to go back to the kitchen, and that's not very private.

After a few false starts, I did get back into the story I was reading, but when I'd stopped for the night and turned out the light, it was a long time before I managed to get to sleep.

CHAPTER TWENTY-SIX

Isn't it funny how you can trace back bits of dreams to the events of the day before? That night, I had a long, convoluted dream that included a parakeet squawking, "No peach, no peach," over and over while Nadine's landlady dangled a key in front of my eyes and intoned, "One key is the key to everything."

The key connection to the previous day was easy to figure out, but it took me a few minutes to put together the part about the bird and the fact that I'd been disappointed to find we were out of peach yogourt.

By the time I'd showered and was fully awake, the other details of the dream had faded completely away. I towel-dried my hair, brushed it out, slipped on a pair of jeans and a T-shirt, and grabbed a bowl of cereal.

"Are you working today?" Mom asked, coming into the kitchen.

"Tonight. Four until closing," I said.

"How are you finding the job?"

"It's okay. The work isn't bad, and I like the shifts I do with Ben. But Lisa is kind of grouchy most of the time, and Carlotta is practically psycho."

"They're all related, right?"

"Yeah, though you'd never know that Ben was one of them. He's the only nice one of the family."

"He's the one you work with most of the time, isn't he?"

"Yes, thank goodness. I don't think I could stand it if I worked mainly with Carlotta. It's bad enough that she's weird, but she's nasty too."

"That makes things very unpleasant," Mom frowned. "Isn't there someone you could talk to about it?"

"Not really. Lisa runs the place, though it's a family business. And she and Carlotta are cousins, I guess. I know they're both cousins to Ben, so I guess that's what they are to each other too."

"They could both be cousins to Ben, but be sisters to each other," Mom pointed out.

"Possible," I said. "The relationship has never been clear to me, and I don't like to ask questions for fear someone ends up accusing me of being nosey. But they don't look that much alike, and they don't seem very close."

"Well, I guess all you can do is try to make the best of things," Mom said. "I don't like to think of you being treated unkindly there, but I know there are sometimes limits to what a person can do about a situation like that. If it got so that you dreaded the thought of going to work because of it, you'd just have to quit."

"Oh, it's not that bad," I said hastily. "Anyway, it's worth it on payday. It's so cool having a cheque at the end of every week."

"Yes, and you'll be able to put some money away toward university too," Mom said.

I tried to summon an enthusiastic expression for this idea. I guess I'll have to start saving up for when I go away to school eventually — but I just started working and I'd much rather enjoy being able to spend my money for the first few months.

"Oh, Shelby, what's your schedule this weekend? I was thinking of inviting Malcolm and Greg over for dinner one evening if you and Greg are both free."

Malcolm is Greg's father, Dr. Taylor. He's pretty cool, and I usually look forward to seeing him. But with things kind of awkward between me and Greg at the moment, I wasn't all that keen on the idea of doing some big family get-together thing.

"Why don't you and Dad just have Dr. Taylor over this time," I said. "That way if Greg and I want to see a movie or something we won't be stuck here."

"Nice way to put it," Mom said.

"No, I didn't ... you know what I mean."

"Shelby, check to see if we're getting low on eggs, dear." Mom changed the subject, opening a notebook and picking up a pen at the same time.

"Yeah, there are only four left. Are you doing the grocery shopping this morning?" I asked as I shut the egg carton.

"Not a full shopping; I'm just picking up a few things. Why, was there something you wanted?"

"More yogourt. We only have blueberry and vanilla left."

She jotted that down along with the other things on her list.

"I'm heading over to Betts's place pretty soon," I said. "I'll call if we're going anywhere. Otherwise, we're just going to hang out at her house for the day. I'll be home before work, though."

"Well, have a nice time." Mom stuck the list into her purse, which she slung over her shoulder.

"Oh, yeah, do you think you can give me a lift to work tonight?" I asked, remembering the weather announcement I'd heard on the radio a bit earlier. "It's supposed to rain."

"I'm sure that either your father or I can manage that."

I rinsed out my bowl and put it in the sink, then swept the floor, which I had forgotten to do the night before. The phone rang.

"Shelby, I have to cancel on you today," Betts said, her voice quavering. "I'm sorry."

"What's up, Betts?"

"I don't want to talk about it."

"Is it Derek?" I asked, ignoring what she'd just said.

"No, it isn't Derek. It's way worse than that." She began to cry and just barely choked out, "I gotta go," before hanging up.

"Betts, wait …" The dial tone told me it was useless. I briefly considered phoning her back, but that seemed pointless. She'd talk about it when she was ready.

That was the alarming thing, though. Betts is *always* ready to talk — about amost anything. I spent a good half-hour wandering through the house wondering what could have upset her so much that she couldn't even discuss it.

Finally, realizing the futility of trying to figure something like that out without the benefit of any information, I slipped into my sandals and headed out for a walk.

Snatches of my dream came back to me as I made my way in the general direction of Broderick's Gas Bar. I hadn't planned specifically to go see Greg — in fact, I wasn't even sure if he was working this early, though he'd mentioned being scheduled during the day today — but it seems my feet were heading there so I guess that's what I was doing.

If I'd reached Broderick's, Greg and I would probably have had a long talk and worked out the day before's problem. That might have pushed the other thoughts that were apparently trying to surface completely out of my head.

Thank goodness I didn't get there in time for that to happen!

CHAPTER TWENTY-SEVEN

The realization, when it hit me, stopped me in my tracks, though of course it was summer and I wasn't actually *making* any tracks.

I'm not exactly sure how it happened either. It seemed as though things just suddenly clicked together in my head, first one thing and then another. It was like pieces of a puzzle, all falling into place until they began to form a picture.

It was a scary picture too, let me tell you. I kind of tried to turn it around, see it from another angle. I did my best to find the flaw that would make the whole thing unravel or fall apart. Only I couldn't.

"It's just a theory," I reminded myself, actually talking out loud alone on the street. Luckily, no one was around. "It's too crazy to be true. I'm making things up again. Surely it isn't true. But what if it *is*?" I found myself pacing, walking back and forth on the sidewalk, which probably looked as nutty as talking aloud without the benefit of an audience.

I tried to calm myself down and think of what to do. The first thing — and of course the most sensible thing — I thought of was to go to the police. I started in that direction. In fact, I was almost to the station when doubts began to dispel any enthusiasm I felt over sharing my theory with an officer.

"Oranges and peaches, noisy water pipes and keys," I said, expelling air disgustedly. "Who's going to listen to a wild theory like that? And suppose they did, suppose they believed me. What would they look into? It wouldn't likely be Nadine. They'd check out the other thing first, to see if any further investigation was warranted on her disappearance. And that would give her captors time to dispose of her, if they haven't already done that."

They probably had. A cold shudder ran down my spine, in spite of the warmth of the day. I knew it had been over a week since Nadine had vanished. What were the odds that she was still alive?

"I have to believe that she is," I told myself. "If I stop believing that ..."

I pushed aside any thoughts that she might, in fact, already be dead. The image of her face, smiling while she chatted casually, rose up in my head. She was so young, so alive. Surely no one was evil enough to kill her, not for that kind of reason.

What's a good reason to a killer, though? What do I know about such things? I wanted to start running and keep going until this whole thing was left somewhere far behind. But I couldn't.

If I was right, I was the only chance Nadine had.

I toyed with the idea of going to Greg, but dismissed it faster than I had the notion of talking to the police. There was enough bad feeling between us over this, and besides, he hadn't really believed anything had happened to her. Or if he had at first, he'd become persuaded she was okay after the police had looked into it. Convinced as I was that he'd only gone along with me to humour me I wasn't inclined to involve him any further.

Without Greg as an option, there wasn't anyone for me to go to. I was on my own.

Forming a plan was no easy thing. There were too many things that were wide open, too many unknowns, for me to come up with anything concrete. All I knew for sure was that I *somehow* had to find out an address, get inside, and check it out without being discovered.

The worst thing was that I was going to have to wait until after work tonight to do it. I thought until my head hurt to find a way around that, but there just wasn't one.

The least I could do would be to prepare myself, in case things worked out for me to somehow find my way to the one place I would need to get into — *if* I was to have any hope of getting some sort of evidence, which was what I'd need to ensure the police would reopen the whole investigation.

What that evidence might be, I wasn't one hundred percent sure. I just had to believe there would be something incriminating. The best-case scenario would be finding Nadine's suitcases, full of her things, which shouldn't be too hard to locate. If those had been disposed of, then I'd just have to poke around a bit harder.

I headed for the hardware store. There, I purchased a glass cutter, a suction cup, and a flashlight. For good measure, I added some pieces of wire, a penknife, and the loudest whistle they had, just in case.

When I got back home, I packed my purchases into a small overnight bag. I threw in a multi-head screwdriver of Dad's and then added Mom's cell phone, making a mental note to mention it to her just before I left for work. The less time she had to wonder why I needed it, the better. I was pretty sure I could come up with a reasonable excuse that wouldn't require any out-and-out lying.

I knew I looked as though something was up, so I was glad to have the excuse of telling Mom that Betts had cancelled our day's plans and that she'd been upset, though I didn't know why. Just as I'd hoped, Mom read my mood as concern for my friend. She offered some helpful advice, which I didn't hear at all.

At last it was time to go to work. Mom drove me there because by that time it was drizzling lightly.

"I think I'm going to be pretty late tonight," I said as we pulled into the parking lot of The Steak Place. "I brought your cell phone with me so I can call a cab after I'm done. Lisa is so grouchy these days that I don't want to have to ask her if I can use the restaurant's phone, even for something like that."

"Why will you be so late?" Mom asked. "Is there a late party here or inventory or something?"

"I'm not really sure what's happening," I said (which was, you must admit, practically the truth). "I just know I'll be later than normal. Don't wait up."

"All right. Well, have a good night then."

I knew Mom would wait until I was in the door before she left. When I reached it I turned and waved. I felt a pang of guilt as she smiled and waved back. I don't usually hide things from my folks or lie to them.

It bothered me a lot that I was deceiving my mom, but there seemed no way around it. If I'd told her what I was up to she'd have hauled me back into the car and taken me straight home.

I wondered how I was going to act natural at work all evening, knowing what I'd be doing as soon as the place was closed for the night.

Chapter Twenty-Eight

Ben looked up with a smile when I pushed through the doors into the kitchen. I smiled back and hoped I looked normal.

"Your folks throw you out?" he joked, seeing the overnight bag I was carrying.

I didn't think I could force a laugh in my present mood, so I nodded sadly and said, "I guess I should have cleaned my room after all," as I dropped the bag casually into the corner.

"Young people nowadays," he shook his head in mock sorrow. "I don't know what will become of you."

"It's hard to say," I said as I pulled my apron on. Turning to the first task of the day, I began to clean up the dishes that had accumulated throughout the afternoon. For once I wished they were piled sky high. I'd have loved to have something that would keep me busy and help the time pass quickly.

It also wouldn't hurt to avoid conversations with Ben and Lisa. I was sure that the fact that I was up to something was written all over my face, and it wouldn't do to have anyone see it and stop me.

It wasn't that busy, though, and I'm not sure how the evening finally dragged to a close. For a while, it had seemed as though it would go on forever.

Oddly enough, when the doors were locked and we were all finishing up our shift-end tasks, I found myself wishing that the hours had continued to stretch ahead. Now that the time for action had arrived, I felt my knees grow weak and my nerve began to fail me. It was only the thought of Nadine that gave me enough courage to go on.

The second I'd finished my work, I pretended to call for a drive, said goodnight to everyone, and slipped out the side door, glancing around to see where the truck I was going to need to sneak into was parked.

I saw it right away, in a spot in the empty lot across the road. I tossed my bag in and then crawled up and over the tailgate and into the back, secure that I was hidden well by the fibreglass cap. Even so, I huddled down in a corner, my heart pounding with fear.

I need not have worried. He came along soon afterward, climbed in, started the engine, and drove off. We hit a few bumps as the truck found potholes in the road, which jarred me and made me rise and then plop back down. I hoped and prayed that it wasn't noticeable up in the front of the truck.

Watching through the open back of the cap, I tried to keep track of where we were turning and what streets we were on. You'd think, having lived in Little River my whole life, that it would have been easy. It wasn't.

For one thing, it was dark, in spite of the streetlights that blinked every so many feet. For another, I wasn't used to seeing things backward, driving around at night in the back of a truck, with a possible kidnapper at the wheel. As unnerved as I was, it's a wonder I could still say with any certainty that I was in my hometown.

Somewhere in the back of my mind was the thought that I had invented the whole thing. I think that might be what kept me from leaping out of the truck and taking off running at the first stop sign we came to.

I didn't have to remind myself that it was still possible that Nadine was perfectly all right, that there'd been no crime, and that the worst thing that could happen would be that I'd be discovered and end up having made a big fool of myself.

On the other hand, if I was right and Nadine had indeed been dragged from her apartment in the dead of night, I was putting myself in the greatest danger imaginable. I tried to remember why going to the police had seemed like such a bad idea, or why I'd thought I could pull this whole thing off.

By the time the truck pulled into a driveway and the headlights shut off, I was a wreck — and it wasn't from the jostling around I'd taken over the rough roads either.

Too late for any of that, I told myself firmly. Just get inside, take a quick look around, and get back out. Of course, I couldn't do that until after the inhabitants of the house were asleep.

My watch told me I'd been scrunched up in the corner of the truck for nearly an hour when I finally stretched out a bit, moved my limbs enough to get them working properly again, and got out of the vehicle. The last light had gone out in the house about twenty minutes before. All I could hope was that no one was still awake in there.

The driveway was to the left of the house, and there was only one basement window facing that direction. I crouched down and crept over to it, shining my flashlight in through the murky pane.

All I saw was a typical basement room, empty except for a few boxes and an old table stuck in the corner. I clicked my flashlight off and snuck around to the back of the house.

Repeating my exploration with two more windows back there, I discovered a furnace room and another room with gardening supplies stacked along the wall. I shone the light around in there carefully, looking for a shovel, hoping I wouldn't see one. I didn't.

Heart pounding furiously, I continued around to the other side. I'd seen that a veranda stretched across the front of the house, so I knew that the window I saw there was the last one.

The thing about this window that was different from the others was that it had been closed in with boards. Clicking my flashlight back on, I saw that they were old and grey, weathered from years of exposure to the elements.

I thought briefly about trying to pry them loose with my penknife, though I wasn't sure the little blade was up to the task. It seemed a bit pointless though, since these weren't new boards. Whatever the reason was that they'd been put there, it hadn't occurred in the past few weeks. Probably a broken window from years gone by, I decided.

I did my best to peer in past them anyway, shining my light through the tiny slits between them, and then trying to perform a miracle by bending the light around their white edges at the sides of the windows. It didn't take any time at all to realize I wasn't going to be able to see into that room.

I returned to the backyard, where there was the best cover against anyone who might happen along. Not only was I hidden from the street, but the streetlight was essentially blocked by the house, so the whole area remained quite dark. A quick check of the time told me that I'd spent about fifteen minutes looking around the outside. I wondered if I was stalling and if, in fact, I even had the necessary daring to go in there.

I also questioned my own judgement one last time, holding a brief debate on whether or not I was creating something that didn't exist. Then a thought came to me. I shone my light around the backyard. It was empty except for a few small bushes that stood here and there in grass that could stand mowing. As I was doing that, an even more important realization hit me. I went back to the boarded window and danced my light over it again, wondering how I'd missed something so important the first time.

I hurried to the back of the house once more, knelt at a window, and reached into my bag. I drew out the glass cutter and suction cup then took a deep breath and tried to steady my nerves.

"Okay," I said, "it's now or never."

Chapter Twenty-Nine

Just as I was getting started, I realized there was something else I needed to do first. Leaving my bag, I skirted along the driveway, on the other side of the truck, and out to the street. The nearest corner was a few houses away. I tried to look casual as I made my way toward it, but it wasn't easy.

As soon as I got there and read the sign that told me what street I was on, I turned around and hurried back, noting the house number just before I made my way behind it again.

The glass cutter was harder to use than I'd expected. After attaching the suction cup to one of the window panes at the back of the house, I'd sliced in a sort of circular pattern around it, going over and over the line I'd made until my wrist hurt. Even so, the piece of glass didn't come out the way I'd thought it would.

Tense and drenched in sweat, I tugged and pushed on the suction cup a few times, which was when it started to feel as though it might be loosening after all. I kept working at it, jiggling and twisting until suddenly it cracked and pulled away. The chunk of glass attached to the cup wasn't exactly the same as I'd cut — its edges were rough and jagged in places. Still, it was out and that was the main thing.

The window clasp, which I'd observed earlier with my flashlight, was a standard affair, the kind that you turn in a half circle to lock in place. It was a few seconds' effort to reach through the opening I'd just made and unlatch it. Then, holding my breath, as though that would make the whole thing quieter, I pulled up on the window as gently as I could.

It resisted at first, then slowly creaked upward. The opening it made was big enough to crawl through, but barely, and as I lowered myself in backwards, bag in hand, I had a strange feeling that I was trapping myself.

It's going to be a lot harder getting back up there to get out, I thought as my feet landed on the floor with a soft thud. I wasn't really worried that anyone would hear, since the two stories suggested the bedrooms would be on the second floor, but the thought that leaving might be a bigger challenge than I'd anticipated worried me.

I walked quickly and quietly through the room I was in, which happened to be the one with the garden supplies, and out into an open area in the centre of the basement. I felt turned around somehow, and it took a few seconds to figure out which side of the house had sported the boarded-up window.

A door stood closed along that wall, with a padlock hanging from a thick metal clasp. As I got closer, I saw that the key was actually sticking out of it, which would have made me smile if I hadn't been so nervous.

Clearly, the reason for the lock was not to prevent someone from going into the room, but to keep someone or something inside from getting out. I turned the key and felt the click as the lock opened then, slid it off the clasp and dropped it into my pocket.

Trembling badly, I pushed the door open and stepped inside, my light trained on the floor. Even in the dim light created by the single beam, I saw her immediately.

She lay on a cot, her hands and feet bound and with a strip of cloth gagging her, pulled tightly and tied behind her head. Her eyes were closed and in the pale light she seemed almost transparent — or pale in death. I choked back a sob and stepped closer, swallowing hard in relief as I saw the steady rise and fall of her chest.

"Nadine," I whispered, touching her as gently as I could. It took a few nudges, each one a bit firmer, before she stirred. When she did, her eyes fluttered open briefly, fell closed again, and then reopened slowly, as though it caused her tremendous effort.

"I'm going to take this off," I whispered, motioning to her gag. "You have to be quiet, though. Do you understand?"

She inclined her head slightly to show she did and I tugged at the knots, which held firm. Not wanting to waste any more time, I pulled out the little penknife and cut through the cloth. It fell to the side.

"Shelby?" she said, her voice a rasping whistle.

"Yes, it's really me," I said softly. I could see that she was both confused and disbelieving, unable to grasp the idea that there was actually someone else there with her.

As I spoke, I worked at the knots on the ropes that bound her hands and feet. My knife would have taken forever to cut through them so I figured it would be fastest to undo them, but they were tight and had apparently been tied by someone who knew what they were doing.

"They ... got ... you ... too?" Panic swept over her face.

"No," I hissed quickly. It wouldn't do to have her cry out in alarm, though by the weakened sound of her voice, she probably couldn't make enough noise to wake someone in the next room. "They don't know I'm here. I'm going to get help."

"Don't," she whimpered. "Don't ... leave .... me."

"I won't," I agreed at once, though every instinct in me screamed to get out. My fingers were sweating as I finally freed her feet, loosening the rope that was connected to the one that bound her wrists.

I was working on getting her hands free when we heard it, the sound of footfalls on the steps. I thought I would faint from fear as they hurried toward the room where we were. I grabbed my bag and rolled under the cot, knowing full well it was not going to hide me from whoever was coming. My hand snaked inside, searching for the cell phone, but there was no time to make a call.

Too late I realized I should have phoned for help the second I'd found her, instead of trying to get her untied and out of there on my own. Fear had muddied my thinking, and I couldn't even imagine what that mistake might cost us.

The door swung open and light burst into the room.

"Well, well, what have we here?"

Stupidly, I'd squeezed my eyes shut, as though that could block out reality. At Ben's voice, I opened them again and saw him leaning down and looking directly at me.

"You wouldn't listen," he sighed and shook his head sadly, as though he was explaining something to a small, exasperating child.

"Ben, I ..." My words broke off. What was there to say?

"Who is it?" Another voice, sharper, joined us.

Behind Ben, I saw that Lisa had come into the room. She too leaned down; she too saw me.

"Come out from under there," she commanded angrily.

I was in no position to argue. I crawled out and immediately cried out, "Please don't hurt me! Please don't kill me!"

"Hush, hysterical girl," Lisa snapped. She took me by the shoulders and shook me.

"I told you," Ben said, turning to his cousin. "I told you it was a mistake to let her live." He gestured with perfect indifference toward Nadine. "Now there are two. We can't possibly stick with the original plan."

"You can't get away with this." I forced bravado into my voice. "You can't, because, because, well, uh, because the police are on their way."

"Oh, really?" Ben smirked. "Did you hear, Lisa? The police are coming."

"They are!" I insisted. "They'll be right here any second now."

"Then why didn't they come *with* you?"

I wondered how I'd ever thought Ben was a nice fellow. His lip was curled in a sneer that made him both ugly and scary to look at, but it was his eyes that told me what he really was. Cold and hard, they looked at me and somehow looked through me at the same time. I knew he would do whatever he thought needed to be done, and without a second's compunction.

"The police are so coming!" I said loudly, knowing full well that the lie was obvious in every word I said. "I, I even told them the address."

"Oh, no, not the address," Ben scoffed. "Now I'm frightened. Now I really believe that the police are going to drive in any second."

"I *do* know the address," I insisted. I knew my voice sounded desperate and pathetic, and that he wasn't buying it. "It's ... it's 197 Marswarble Way."

"Bravo," Ben said, clapping his hands slowly. "But you're lying. No one is coming."

"Ben, be quiet. This is a serious problem." Lisa spoke again, and there was something in her voice that made me look at her closer.

To my surprise her eyes were troubled. In fact, her whole expression seemed burdened, as though she'd just been given some terrible news she didn't want to accept, but had to.

"Don't let him hurt us," I said to her.

But she was already turning away, forcing herself to walk from the room, her shoulders stiff.

"This is Ben's show. I can't do anything to help you," she said as she exited the doorway. "I'm sorry."

And then Ben was coming toward me, a length of rope in his hands.

"Might as well make this easy on yourself," he said casually. "The more you struggle, the more I'm going to have to hurt you."

CHAPTER THIRTY

"How did you know I was here?" I asked Ben, trying to stall. "I was really quiet."

"How?" He threw his head back and laughed. "Did you think there'd be nothing set up to warn me of intruders? How stupid do you think I am?"

"But I didn't hear any alarms or anything."

"Nothing so unreliable as alarms, which any decent burglar can disable in no time," he said, taking one of my hands and starting to wrap rope around it. "I prefer the old canine system, only with dogs that are trained to be silent. Instead of barking their fool heads off, my dogs listen and watch, and if they hear anything they come to me and let me know. So, I am warned, but the intruder is not. Clever, what?"

I wasn't much in the mood to admire his cleverness, especially since at that moment he was holding my hands together while he wound rope around my wrists. Beside us, on the cot, Nadine gave a small murmur of protest but made no attempt to move.

"What are you going to do with us?" I asked, trying to look him right in the eye.

"Now, that's the sad part," he said. From the tone of his voice, you'd have sworn he really felt bad about it. "You see, Nadine here was going to be allowed to live. But your interference means you must both die. See what has happened because you just wouldn't let it go?"

I kicked at him and tried to twist away from his firm grasp, but it was useless. He held the rope that bound my wrists tightly with one hand while the other rose and came toward me. The slap, even though I saw it coming, was a shock, which is kind of amusing when you think about it. After all, it shouldn't be a huge surprise that someone who's willing to kill you might hit you too.

"You'll be more cooperative soon enough," he said pleasantly. "Just like our little Nadine here."

The full meaning of his words didn't hit me until a few moments later when Lisa returned. By then, my hands and feet had been tied and he was replacing the ropes I'd removed from Nadine.

"We need a gag for this one." Ben addressed Lisa, nodding in my direction.

"I can only do one thing at a time," she said. Her eyes flashed angrily at him, and I wondered if it was because he was ordering her around or because she was upset by what was being done to us.

I saw then what she held in her hand and understood why Ben had told me I'd soon be more cooperative. A syringe filled with clear liquid came toward me, and though I squirmed, she plunged it into my thigh easily.

The effect was almost instant. A warm, sleepy feeling crawled through me, leaving me groggy and almost confused. I tried to say something, but my tongue felt thick and awkward, with a life of its own.

No wonder Nadine had been incoherent and unable to say much when I'd taken off her gag earlier. She'd been drugged, floating in the same state of unreality that I now drifted in.

Ben and Lisa were talking, but they seemed very far away, their words muffled and disconnected. I had no idea what they were saying, although it seemed to be an argument of some sort.

And really, what did I care? It suddenly made no difference at all what they did to me, to us. I think, at that moment, Ben could have brought in a gun and shot me and I'd just have lain there not caring what was happening.

Even in the state I was in, I had enough reasoning power left to realize that as long as they kept me drugged like this, I would be totally unable to do anything to help myself or Nadine. Heck, not only could I not *do* anything, I couldn't even clearly *think* anything.

That was unfortunate for Lisa, because she chose that very time to grill me. Since she'd just given me the injection, you'd have thought she'd know better, but she didn't. She just forged ahead.

"Shelby, it's me, Lisa," she said, leaning down. "I want to help you."

Well, I wasn't *that* gone that I didn't know who she was! I smiled crookedly and nodded to show I understood. Oddly, a feeling of great affection for her swept over me.

"First, I have a few questions I need to ask you. Then I can help you."

"Okay," I said dreamily. It echoed in my head, the "k" thick and guttural.

"How did you know?"

"Knowaaa?" I asked, then tried again. "Know. Whaa...t?"

"That Nadine was here with us. How did you figure it out?" She smiled and patted my arm. "It was very clever of you. I'm just curious how you put it all together."

My head played flashes of images and I tried to connect them, but it wasn't working so well.

"Thu pies," I slurred at last. That made me giggle, because I'd been trying to say *pipes*, and the expression on her face struck me as hilarious as she tried to figure out what clue I'd gotten from *pies*.

Ben interrupted then, saying something to Lisa about later. She looked reluctant but she withdrew, patting my arm again. "We'll talk after," she said, "you just rest for now."

I didn't have a whole lot of options, seeing as I was tied up. It was the gag, which I heard Ben remind Lisa to get, that was going to be the worst, though. My tongue already felt ten times its normal size. I was convinced a gag would choke me to death.

Luckily, I never found out whether or not I was right. Just as Lisa returned with a strip of cloth, a banging came on the door upstairs.

"Police! Open up!" a voice hollered. "Now!"

They didn't wait. Seconds later the door crashed open and we could hear feet running everywhere. Ben and Lisa stood frozen in shock for the first few seconds, and by the time they tried to react it was too late. A couple of officers had rushed downstairs and stood, guns drawn, yelling for them to get their hands up.

Chapter Thirty-One

The next thing I knew Ben and Lisa had been handcuffed and led away. I heard one of the officers say there'd been two more upstairs, which was a surprise. I'd thought Carlotta was the only other one in the house. Even in my hazy state, I could recall Ben telling me that the three of them were sharing a place while the family business got off the ground.

Then I heard sirens, which I thought was kind of strange. After all, the police had already caught the bad guys, you wouldn't think they'd need more.

Only it wasn't police. It was a pair of ambulances. They strapped both Nadine and me onto stretchers. They also stuck needles in us for no apparent reason, since they were just short, empty plastic tubes that weren't attached to an IV or anything. After checking a few things like pulse and blood pressure, they loaded us into the ambulances and headed off.

I tried to tell the guy in the back of the ambulance with me that I really needed to go home, and that they could just drop me off there. He said things like "sure kid" and "no problem" but we ended up at the hospital anyway. I wished my tongue was working a bit better so I could have told him that I didn't appreciate being humoured or having my hopes raised for nothing.

I was dismayed to see Mom and Dad come rushing in shortly afterward, while I was still waiting for a doctor to come and check me out.

Mom cried a lot. Dad held onto her, sort of holding her up with one arm, but he looked kind of scared and on the verge of crumbling himself.

I figured I was in *big* trouble.

The doctor came then and he checked me out, repeating some of the things the ambulance guys had done, and adding a few of his own. He tried to reassure Mom and Dad, but it was a bit difficult since Mom still wasn't exactly what you'd call settled down.

"Her vitals are fine. We're just going to keep an eye on her for the night," he kept saying, and Mom kept right on crying and kind of trembling.

After a bit they moved me upstairs to a room and my folks came in and sat with me. I was really woozy and all I wanted to do was sleep, but I figured I'd better try to stay awake and talk to my folks, seeing as they'd gotten up out of bed in the middle of the night to come down there.

I tried to tell them I was sorry. It came out all weird and garbled, which didn't do much to cheer up poor Mom. I think she figured I was fried for life or something. She kept saying "Oh, Randall," in the most pathetic way, and I'd have sure liked to tell her it was all right, but every time I tried to talk it seemed to make things a bit worse.

At last one of the nurses came in and told them I was doing fine and that the best thing would be for them to go home and get some sleep and let me get some rest. Once they'd taken the advice and left I was out like a light.

In the morning I woke up feeling sort of off, if you know what I mean. I still couldn't quite focus or concentrate properly, and my head hurt a little, but I could tell I was on the way back to being myself.

The doctor came by again, only this time he didn't do anything except talk. He said some embarrassing stuff like he hadn't realized he had a real live hero as a patient and other dumb things like that. He wanted to know how I was feeling and then he said I could go home whenever my parents came to get me.

I asked him how Nadine was, and he told me she was fine and why didn't I go down the hall and see for myself.

I didn't have a housecoat or anything with me but the nurse brought me another one of the strange night-gowns they give you in hospitals, the kind with the back wide open except for a couple of ties, which I was already wearing. I put the second one on backward and then walked three rooms down the hall to the room the nurse told me Nadine was in.

She was barely awake, but she sat up as soon as I got to the doorway of her room. She started crying and held her arms out. As soon as I was close enough, she grabbed onto me and hugged me just about as hard as Mom and Dad had last night.

"I don't know *how* you did it," she sobbed, "but you saved my life."

"Aw, Ben told me they weren't planning to kill you until I interfered," I said, though I was pretty sure he'd been lying.

Her answer surprised me, though. She told me, in faltering terms, that she'd heard Ben and Lisa talking about what to do with her. Can you imagine anything as cruel as talking right in front of someone about whether or not you should kill them?

"Ben kept saying they should just get rid of me," she said, "like I was just some old disposable thing they didn't need around. It was actually Lisa who begged and persuaded him that they should let me live. Only, the plan they came up with wasn't much better than killing me, really."

"What was the plan?" I asked, still grappling with the horror that all of this had been discussed in her presence.

"They were sending me back to the city with some guy who came here a day or two ago. And he was supposed to keep me locked up there and get me hooked on heroin — turn me on to it, Lisa called it — and then put me on the street as a prostitute. Ben actually made jokes about how well I'd fit into this guy's stable.

"I'm pretty sure I was supposed to be leaving with him today," she continued, pausing as a shudder ran through her. "If you hadn't found me when you did — my whole life would have been totally ruined."

"So *that* was the fourth person in the house," I said. "Well, the police got them all. Speaking of police, I imagine they'll need statements from us. Besides what they did to you, we'll have to fill them in on what this whole thing was about."

"I wouldn't mind hearing that myself."

I turned to see Greg standing in the doorway.

CHAPTER THIRTY-TWO

My knees went weak at the unexpected sight of Greg there in the hospital. Though I managed a smile and a hello, both were pretty feeble.

I tried to read his expression, but his face was set in a hard line, as if he'd clamped his jaw tight.

"Your mom called me," he said at last, like he didn't know what else to say.

"Well, good then. I'm glad she did."

"So, do you want to tell me what happened?"

I told him about hiding in Ben's truck and going to the house and finding Nadine. "I almost persuaded myself I was wrong and didn't go inside at all," I added, "until I realized a couple of things. One was that they had a bunch of gardening supplies in a basement room, but there was no sign of any gardening anywhere in the yard. The second was that there was a window recently boarded up. I almost missed that because the boards were all old and grey from the weather. It took a few moments before I clued in to the fact that the ends of them were white, which meant they'd been newly cut."

I told him about the injection Lisa had given me and the police coming and the ambulance drive to the hospital — what I could remember of it anyway.

"Who called the police?" he asked.

"Oh, that was me," I smiled. "I had Mom's cell phone with me and when I heard someone coming, I had just enough time to dial 911. I left it open, out of sight under the cot, and kind of yelled so the emergency operator could hear me."

"But they were right there in the room with you, weren't they? It didn't make them suspicious when you started saying stuff that would get the police to come?"

"Well, I started off by yelling for them please not to kill me, or something like that, so the person on the other end of the phone would keep listening." I explained how I'd managed to work in the address of the place so the police would know where to go.

"Wow, that was pretty smart," Greg said. His face was relaxing a bit. "How did you know where Nadine was, though?"

"Believe it or not, I think the nutty landlady actually helped there. I think she must have heard something the night that Ben went to Nadine's apartment, something that told her what this was all about. Being obsessed with Julie Andrews movies, she made an association with a film that's got some weird similarities to what happened here.

"Another thing, Nadine's suitcases were packed and taken out after I told Ben I'd been in there and nothing was missing. That was what prevented the police from looking into her disappearance, and it happened right after I talked to Ben. It was almost like I'd given him a suggestion without meaning to.

"I missed the connection at the time because it hadn't occurred to me that Ben might have something to do with Nadine being missing."

"But *why?*" Greg asked then. "What was his motive?"

"Okay, let me take you through it from the start. First thing, I had this dream about keys and peaches. Specifically, a single key. That's the first thing that clicked into place for me.

"You see, once when I was working with Nadine, she had to turn on the cash register to take a customer's payment. In fact, it was the guy who stares at you, Nadine!" I paused and filled her in on what I'd learned from him.

"Anyway, recently, I made a call from the phone by the cash, and Lisa asked me to pass her the key. Except, instead of the ring full of keys that had been there before, it was just a single key. That made me wonder why she'd taken off the others.

"It also reminded me that Nadine had seemed upset her last night at work. I'd assumed it was related to something in her personal life, and it took a long time before I stopped to think it might be something on the job. And that's where the key came in."

"I was just curious," Nadine said softly. "I had no idea."

"Well, as soon as I started thinking on those lines, it all fell into place. Like, Greg, remember the apartment building and the noisy pipes?"

"Yeah, the ones that make the landlady think the apartment is haunted."

"Right. They make noise *every morning* when Mr. Elliot has his shower. It reminded me of the noisy pipes at work, only I realized that the pipes at the restaurant seemed to be making a racket at random times. And the more I thought about it, the more I could see that I'd been hearing the noises at all kinds of irregular times — when *no one had any water turned on*."

"That's weird," Greg said. He looked really interested.

"And there was another thing. I'd seen a case of citrus air freshener, but when I cleaned out the bathrooms, the fresheners in them were peach."

"So, that could just mean that they use two different kinds, couldn't it?"

"They use two kinds all right, only the citrus one can never be smelled inside the place. On the other hand, you can always smell oranges *outside* the staff entrance."

"I guess I've noticed that without thinking anything of it," Greg said.

"Neither did I, until it all fell into place."

I was suddenly exhausted and needed to sit down. The magnitude of everything that had happened over the past few weeks was starting to dawn on me, and the realization of the danger I'd been in the night before was hitting me too.

Greg knelt beside me as I sank into the visitor's chair by Nadine's bed. He stroked my arm gently with his hand. I continued.

"I asked myself, *why* would water be running at odd times? Why would there be air freshener vented to the *outside*? And what might Nadine have seen in the building that would have made it necessary for someone to do something to silence her?"

"And the answer?"

"My guess — a hydroponics operation. An automatic watering system would explain the noises in the pipes when no one had water turned on, and the air freshener vented outside, well, that would cover the smell of the plants.

"I think that they had two businesses going at the same time, using the legitimate one to cover for the illegal one. On top of that, they could use the restaurant to launder money from the drug operation.

"The big back room that they claimed was going to be done over for private banquets and stuff at some point in time was, I believe, actually being used to grow marijuana." I turned to Nadine questioningly, since I was pretty sure she'd seen what was in there.

"You're right Shelby, but you want to know something really funny?" Nadine asked with a rueful smile. "I did peek in the back room, just out of curiosity, and I did see a bunch of plants. Only, I didn't even know what they were. Ben caught me and his reaction kind of scared me but I thought he was just mad that I looked in there without permission. I didn't even know what I'd seen.

"Then Ben came to my place right after work that night, just as I was getting a snack. He was acting natural, but I had a feeling that something was wrong." She shuddered with the memory. "He insisted on coming in, said he had something to give me, but that was just a trick."

"Did he happen to have a pop with him?" I asked, remembering the spilled cola in her living room.

"Yeah, in fact, I remember how that made it all seem pretty normal, him standing in the hallway holding a bottle of Coke looking as casual as could be, but it was part of his plan," she said, nodding. "Once he got inside, he spilled some, by 'mistake' of course, but when

I brought in some paper towels and leaned forward to clean it up, he grabbed me from behind.

"He had a cloth with something on it that he held up to my face. Whatever it was, it made me pass out, and when I woke up he had me tied and gagged. He was talking, telling me we were going to take a nice drive, only I wouldn't be coming back. I can't remember what else he said but something made it clear I'd walked into the middle of a drug thing."

"It's weird how you can look right at something and not see it, or recognize what it actually is," I told her. "I did the same thing, focusing on the wrong suspects and nearly missing what was really going on. I guess a person needs to pay more attention to little things that don't fit, even if you don't understand what they mean right away."

I smiled then. "It should cheer you to know that one of the things that proved Ben's undoing was that very bottle of pop. If not for that, I'd probably still be thinking of Leo as the main suspect."

"I wonder why they didn't just grow the marijuana at their house," Nadine mused aloud. "You'd think there'd be less chance of getting found out that way."

"Not necessarily," Greg said. "There'd be the fact that they were using way too much power for a normal household, which is what gets a lot of people caught."

I guess Nadine and Greg and I probably had a lot more to talk about, but Mom and Dad showed up to get me then. They were way beyond relieved when they saw that I wasn't still all looped and dopey. I was kind of hoping that their relief might take away any urge they had to ground me for the rest of my life.

Still, the thought of not leaving my own home for a while was actually pretty appealing at that moment.

Then I remembered that Betts had been upset over something the last time I talked to her. I hoped I'd at least be allowed to go to see her to find out what the problem had been. *Well*, I thought on the drive home, *whatever it is, at least it won't involve some sort of mystery.*

That just goes to show how wrong I can be.

Acknowledgements

The fictional world often springs, either directly or indirectly, from the people and events around us. For this reason, I am indebted to those whose lives touch and bless my own.

My husband, Brent, for his endless love, faith, and support.

My children, Anthony and Pamela, for inspiring me daily.

My parents, Bob and Pauline Russell; my brothers, Danny and Andrew; and their respective partners, Gail and Shelley, for their love and encouragement.

The Sherrards, for being my second family in every sense.

My sixth grade teacher, Alf Lower, for planting the seed that grew.

Others who have been especially supportive include: Janet Aube, Karen Donovan, Ray Doucet, Karen Dyer, Angie Garofolo, Donna Guy, John Hambrook, Sandra Henderson, David Jardine, Marsha Skrypuch, Paul Theriault, Bonnie Thompson, and many of my staff at Glenelg.

At The Dundurn Group, I am sincerely grateful to Kirk Howard, Publisher, and the entire Dundurn team. Particular thanks are due to:

Barry Jowett, Editorial Director and true wit. This story is better for his guidance and suggestions.

Andrea Pruss, Assistant Editor, for knowing all the rules *and* for letting me break one once in a while.

Jennifer Scott, the fabulous Director of Design and Production. Her talents amaze me!

Jennifer Easter (Queen Jen) for many behind-the-scenes efforts, and for a special contribution to this story.

Mike Millar, a fine Publicist and a genuinely nice guy.

And, Vice President Beth Bruder, for fussing over the rest of us.

AGMV Marquis
MEMBER OF SCABRINI MEDIA
Quebec, Canada
2004